PURRFECT CANCEL

THE MYSTERIES OF MAX 78

NIC SAINT

D1525637

PURRFECT CANCEL

The Mysteries of Max 78

Copyright © 2023 by Nic Saint

Edited by Chereese Graves

www.nicsaint.com

Give feedback on the book at: info@nicsaint.com

facebook.com/nicsaintauthor
@nicsaintauthor

First Edition

Printed in the U.S.A

PURRFECT CANCEL

Canceled Anonymous

An epidemic swept through Hampton Cove, and even though I wasn't one of those infected, it still filled me with dread, since several of our nearest and dearest were amongst those taking a hit. The name of the disease was cancelation, and the symptoms were being fired from one's job, banned from one's social circles and generally being turned into an outcast. The victims were many, and the solution hard to come by, especially when our very own human Chase was suspended. Tough to investigate a crime when you're the victim!

I have to admit at first I was a little hesitant to take this whole business seriously, but when Kingman was canceled, and then Shanille, cat choir's conductor, and eventually the entire cat choir, it became obvious that if we didn't take a stand, our entire way of life would be a thing of the past. But who was behind this pernicious campaign, and what could possibly be its objective? Suffice it to say we had our work cut out for us!

CHAPTER 1

Garret Root had been walking his dog with a spring in his step when he thought he heard a voice addressing him. He glanced around to determine the origin of the sound, which is when he saw that a woman of particularly attractive aspect was looking at him intently from a nearby window.

He retraced his steps and plastered his most ingratiating smile onto his face, thrust out his chest as far as it would go without making him look like a duck, sucked in his belly, and said, "Hi there," in his most sonorous tone of voice.

The woman wasn't smiling, though. On the contrary. If his eyes weren't deceiving him, she was actually projecting an active hostility that made him reel. "You should be ashamed of yourself, Garret Root," she said.

He blinked several times in abject astonishment. "Have we met?"

"I should hope not!"

"But... why ashamed? What do you mean?"

"Oh, you know," she said emphatically, giving him the

kind of hard stare that was designed to take the wind out of his sails and alert him to trouble ahead.

"But I don't," he said. "I really don't."

She shook her head, causing her blond tresses, which framed a very lovely face, he couldn't help but notice, to dance around in pleasant abandon. But all the while her eyes remained hard and cold, boring into him like twin gimlets. "I hate it when you do that," she announced.

"Do what?" he asked, still proceeding absolutely mystified.

"Pretend like nothing's happening, when all the while you know perfectly well what you've been up to." She now added an upheld index finger to the mix, wagging it in a reproachful fashion. "Fair warning, Mr. Root. If you don't go to the police right this instant and turn yourself in, I swear to God…"

He gaped at her. "Police?" he said, his voice going a little squeaky at the mention of the constabulary. "What does the police have to do with this?"

"Oh, for crying out loud," she said, and promptly retreated from the window where she had been resting her arm and looking out onto a world that had hitherto seemed hospitable and pleasant but now was quickly becoming less so. She closed the window with a slam, and Garret, already stunned by the accusations leveled against him, felt his heart make a sudden little jump in his chest, which wasn't part of the service that faithful organ had been designed for. Staggering back, he almost bumped into an elderly lady, who had snuck up behind him unseen.

"I've heard every single word, Garret Root!" said the old lady as he whirled around to face her. "And I'll add my two cents by telling you that if you don't turn yourself in, the good citizens of this town will! And that's a promise!"

"But… what did I do?!" he cried, as bewildered as before.

2

"Don't play dumb with me, young man. You know perfectly well what you did!"

"But I don't, I swear!"

She made a soft tsk-tsking sound while shaking her head in abject condemnation at such stubbornness. "There's a word for people like you, but since I'm a God-fearing person, I won't say it out loud. But if you've got one ounce of decency left in you, you will do the right thing. And you will do it now!"

And with these words, she took off at a vigorous pace that belied her age.

He stared after her, wondering if the world had suddenly gone mad as a hatter. The only thing he could think was that this was all a case of mistaken identity, and both the pretty lady and the old woman were mistaking him for someone else entirely. But whoever this other person was, he must have been up to something really terrible to merit being subjected to such a harsh verbal barrage.

But since his conscience was clear, and as far as he could tell he had done nothing wrong since being put into this world thirty-six years, three months and two days ago, he continued his walk into town, his beloved beagle right at his heel. It didn't take the pair long to arrive at their destination, which was the General Store, where Garret intended to buy some necessary items for dinner tonight. But when he walked into the store, he became aware of the same gimlet stare the pretty lady had subjected him to, only this time coming from the store owner, Wilbur Vickery, a man who, even though not the sunniest of personalities, had never been anything but kind to him, a loyal and frequent customer.

"I don't think I want you coming to this store anymore," said Wilbur now.

"But why?" he said.

"You know," said Wilbur darkly. He gestured with an

3

outstretched arm at the entrance to the store. "Out! Right now!"

"But what did I do?" he said plaintively.

"Just leave, before I make you," said Wilbur, inserting a certain measure of menace into his voice, which brooked no contest whatsoever.

And so he exited the store, meek as a lamb, wondering what could possibly be going on here.

For a moment he just stood there, unsure how to proceed, when a loud hissing sound reached his ears. It came from underneath the outside display of veggies and fruits, and as he glanced down in that direction, he saw that Kingman, Wilbur's large cat, was actually hissing at him!

"Sweet kitty," he said quickly, not wanting to be subjected to the cat's claws of steel. "There's a sweet kitty."

And since the whole world seemed to have suddenly turned against him, he hurried away, glancing left and right in a furtive fashion. Before long, he had reached the post office, and as he took a seat on the bench placed in front of the establishment, determined to get his racing heart and mind back under control, a little girl took a seat next to him. She was licking a lollipop and staring at him with the kind of natural curiosity kids possess at that age.

"Are you the man who showed his dingeling to those kids?" she asked.

"What?! No! Of course not!" he said.

"You look like him. His picture was in the paper, you see."

"What picture? What paper? What dingeling!"

"My mom said you showed your dingeling to the kids in your school, and she said that's a very bad thing to do, especially since you're a teacher, and teachers are not supposed to show their dingelings to anyone, and if MY teacher ever showed HIS dingeling to me, I should tell her so she could report him."

"But I never showed my dingeling to anyone!" he cried.

But then suddenly, the little girl's mother emerged from the post office, took one look at him, and grabbed her daughter by the arm, snatching her off the bench. "You, sir, should be ashamed of yourself," she snapped. "Let's go, Carly." And as they walked away, she said in an admonishing fashion, "How many times have I told you never to talk to strangers?"

"But he's not a stranger, Mommy," said the little girl. "He's the dingeling man."

Garret now noticed how his mouth was slightly agape and made the effort to close it. He was the dingeling man? His picture was in the paper? But how? And when? And since the newsstand was right across the street, he was off that bench and crossing the street in a heartbeat. It was with trembling fingers that he picked up a paper from the stand. Plastered across the front page was his face! And above it, the headline screamed, 'SICK PERVERT CAUGHT IN THE ACT!' Underneath it, in smaller print, it specified, 'Garret Root—Most Hated Man In America?'

CHAPTER 2

J'd been playing with a mouse as a form of entertainment when all of a sudden the mouse scooted underneath the couch, and try as I might, I couldn't catch it.

Before you judge me, let me make a couple of things perfectly clear: the mouse wasn't an actual living, breathing creature but one of those mechanical gizmos that are self-propelled and available from any fine online store. And the entertainment aspect wasn't for my own benefit but for that of Grace, our human's little human, who seemed to enjoy that kind of thing. Or at least that's what Odelia had told us. And so the four of us—myself, Dooley, Harriet, and Brutus—had been taking turns to provide this entertainment Grace seemed to crave so much.

"Max, what are you doing?" asked Harriet.

"I'm trying to find that mouse," I said, reaching underneath the couch to retrieve the little gizmo.

"It popped out the other side," Brutus informed me, "and is going hell for leather in the direction of the kitchen."

"Look at it go," said Dooley. "I think it's going to make the great escape."

The four of us lined up to stare at the thing as it raced across the floor.

"It's going for the pet flap," said Brutus, surprise in his voice.

"That's impossible," I said. "It's a mechanical mouse, not an animal."

"I'm telling you, it's going to try and escape," said our friend.

As we watched on, I saw that he was correct in his estimation of the gizmo's intentions. For some odd reason it was making a beeline for the pet flap. A couple more feet and it would be out the door and out in the great outdoors, and who knows where it might go next. New York? Florida? Albuquerque? The world was its oyster. But just then, Gran entered the kitchen via that same kitchen door, and even as we shouted, "Gran, watch out!" she stepped right on top of the mouse.

There was a sort of crunching sound, and as Gran lifted her foot to look at the thing, it was clear that whatever grand designs it had made would have to be put on hold for the nonce. Clearly the pep had gone out of its step.

"Oh, that poor thing," said Dooley, who has probably the biggest heart of the four of us. "We have to take it to Vena to get it fixed."

"It's just a gizmo, Dooley," I said. "Not a real mouse."

"Max is right," said Brutus. "What it needs is a toymaker, not a vet."

"Maybe Chase can fix it?" Dooley suggested. "Odelia never stops saying how handy he is with his hands."

This statement elicited a smile from the three of us. "Chase might be handy," said Harriet. "But I have a feeling this thing is permanently out of commission."

"What are you trying to pull?" said Gran, who didn't look entirely pleased at the state of affairs. "Are you trying to get me killed?" She then directed her ire at her great-grand-daughter. "Please keep your toys in your toy box," she said. "Unless you want me to trip and fall."

But Grace wasn't impressed. Lately, she had taken to her tablet and studying stuff on there. "Did you know that energy equals mass times the speed of light squared?" she now asked.

We all turned to take her in. "No, I did not know that," I said, having no idea what she was talking about. "But I do know that your mouse is out of commission."

She made a throwaway gesture with her hand. "Oh, who cares about some silly mouse. I only did that to keep you guys entertained."

"Odd," said Harriet. "We thought we were keeping you entertained."

She planted a hand on her hip and made a comical face. "Now why would I find such a terrible pastime entertaining? In my personal opinion, these blood sports should be outlawed."

We shared a look of surprise. "What blood sports? What do you mean?" asked Harriet.

"Cats chasing mice, of course. It's so cruel there should be a law against it. Now take a seat and I'll tell you all about quantum mechanics. Now *that* is what I call entertainment."

Frankly, I had a feeling quantum mechanics was just about as entertaining as watching paint dry, and after Grace had started educating us on the basic tenets of this science, I discovered that my hunch had been correct. The upshot was that the four of us were fast asleep by the time she reached the quantum part of quantum mechanics, which I guess is at least something positive about it. When Gran joined us on the couch, I was dreaming about a mean army of mechanical mice declaring war on all cats and attacking us with their weapons of mouse destruction.

I woke up with a shiver, and realized that Gran had been talking to us.

"I said, 'There should be a law against people like that,'" she repeated.

"People like what?" I asked as I yawned.

"Like this guy Garret Root, of course. First he exposes himself to a bunch of kids on the playground, and then my son simply allows him to walk free!" She slammed the palm of her hand with her fist. "I know what we'll do. We'll keep an eye on that guy from now on. This is exactly what the neighborhood watch was designed for. Who's with me for the first watch?"

"Who's Garret Root?" asked Dooley.

"Only the most hated man in America," said Gran. "And he just happens to live in Hampton Cove. So as I see it, it's our sacred duty to keep an eye on the guy and make sure he isn't up to his horrible old tricks again. So who's with me?"

When none of us responded—mainly due to the fact that we had just enjoyed a pleasant nap and weren't ready to engage with the world at the drop of a hat—her expression turned sour.

"Okay, I get the message." She got up with an alacrity that belied her age. "But next time you need something, don't come crying to me, you hear!" And with these words, she was off, gently simmering with barely suppressed resentment.

"Did Gran say something?" asked Harriet.

"Where did she go off to?" asked Brutus.

"She mentioned something about the watch," said Dooley.

Which just goes to show that quantum mechanics may be all right for some, but it can lead to an unexpected outcome for others. Which just might be one of its basic tenets. I'd ask Grace, but she had fallen asleep herself.

And so we followed her example and picked up our naptus interruptus by returning to the land of Nod. At least this time there wasn't an army of mechanical mice trying to murder me in my sleep!

CHAPTER 3

*J*im Root studied his appearance in the full-length mirror. The suit the salesgirl had foisted on him didn't look too shabby, he had to admit. It wasn't entirely his style, but it was certainly the kind of classic and understated look his sister and the rest of his family would appreciate. His first inclination when Cristy had invited him to the wedding had been to rent a tux, as he had done for all the other weddings—and funerals—he had been invited to in recent years. But then simple economics had told him that buying one was probably the more common-sense solution. And so he had set out to his local fashion emporium to acquire for himself such an item of clothing.

He would have preferred to get a snazzy suit in checkered black-and-yellow or a loud pink or purple, of course. Or something along the lines of what Ryan Gosling would wear to the premiere of one of his hit movies. But since he was neither suicidal nor Ryan Gosling, he had settled for the charcoal specimen he was modeling now. His sister would kill him if he showed up looking like something out of a fashion magazine. A very classic girl in every sense of the word, she wouldn't appreciate if her big brother upset the apple cart in such a way and dragged the attention away from herself and her new husband, who was something big in insurance if Jim's recollection wasn't deceiving him. He had to admit he wasn't all that interested in his sister's latest catch, since chances were that he wouldn't be around long enough to get to know the guy. It was Cristy's third marriage in the last ten years, and already she and her betrothed were fighting like cats and dogs, if their mother's words were to be believed.

"I like it," he told the salesgirl. "I'll take it."

He had glanced at the price tag and even though it was a little above what he had budgeted for such an expense, if Cristy kept up her streak of failed marriages, he would get some good mileage out of the suit for her next three weddings over the course of the next ten years. And if she did keep divorcing her husbands at the standard rate, there might even be a couple of funerals amongst their relatives, who got upset each time Cristy threw another one of her husbands under the bus.

It wasn't that Cristy was a difficult woman to get along with—anything but. It was that she had such awful taste in men that she kept picking losers. Even when she was still dating, she had come home with the kinds of boyfriends no parent could possibly approve of, and even though all of her friends told her not to go for the same type, Cristy persisted, convinced as she was that if you simply keep plugging away, at some point you will magically hit upon Mr. Right. In other words, she was a firm believer in the law of numbers as applied to dating.

The salesgirl wrapped up the suit, and he paid for the item with his company credit card, which hadn't seen this much action for quite a while. Then he tucked the package under his arm and walked out of the store, happy that he could tick off this item on his extensive to-do list. Cristy had been so wise not to tap her brother as best man this time, opting to go with one of her dubious friends instead. During one of her previous marriages, the groom had been completely wasted, and instead of making sure the man stood in front of the altar all sobered up and ready to go, Jim had been so busy arranging some last-minute deal that he had neglected this crucial part of his best-man duties and had allowed the guy to sleep off his bender in the confessional before becoming aware of the distinct dearth of grooms of any description when his sister had cried buckets, convinced that she had been stood up. In due course, the groom had been retrieved, positioned on his marker, and prompted to deliver his lines at the right time.

The wedding had lasted twenty-four hours before Cristy had thrown a giant temper tantrum and demanded a divorce. Turned out the guy had slept with one of her bridesmaids on the eve of the wedding—an unforgivable offense.

He walked with rapid steps in the direction of his car, threw the suit onto the passenger seat before taking up position behind the wheel. Today was a big day. His business had been struggling for months, but finally he had managed to turn it around by finding a new niche in the market. One of his early clients had seen an opportunity and now they were meeting to talk turkey and a potential massive injection of capital. And as nervousness started to take hold of him, he made a conscious effort to slow down his breathing, stop his heart from beating a hundred-and-twenty beats per minute, and make sure he was calm and collected for the upcoming meeting, which was due to take place in half an hour at the Star Hotel.

This was it. If he pulled this off, he might be able to save his company from ruin. And since he had so much riding on this deal, he knew he had to present the best version of himself. Be the best he could be. So he gripped the steering wheel tightly, popped the CD in the CD player with the motivational message from the number-one motivational business coach, and as he listened to the man drone on about thinking positive thoughts and working through a list of motivational exercises, he pulled his car away from the curb and into traffic. And as he did, a call came in. He quickly checked the display and saw that it was his sister Cristy.

He closed his eyes. Oh, dear. Not now!

But he couldn't very well ignore his little sister, especially on the eve of her wedding.

"Hey, sis," he said after he tapped a button on his steering wheel. "What's up?"

Immediately, he could sense that something was terribly wrong. "It's Clint," Cristy said in a weepy voice, referring to her future husband. "I've just discovered that he's part of a very nasty group of people."

Oh dear, oh dear, oh dear. "What group of people?"

"Pet torturers!"

He frowned. "Pet torturers? What do you mean?"

"Clint is part of a group of people who share images of pets being tortured, Jim. The man is a monster! A psycho! A freak!"

"I'm sure there's a perfectly reasonable explanation," he said.

"No, there isn't. It's all right there in horrific detail! He's part of a group called Masters of the Universe, and torturing pets is part of their initiation ritual."

"So what does this initiation consist of, exactly?" he asked, though he really didn't want to know.

She took a deep breath. "They have to pick a pet, and then they have to torture that pet, and then they have to take pictures and post them in their group as evidence."

"That is sick," he said, his stomach turning as he listened.

"It's all part of their philosophy. That only weak people would ever think there's anything wrong with establishing your mastery over an inferior species!"

"You should go to the police, Cris. The man is obviously some kind of psycho."

"Oh, I'm going," she assured him. "And I'm exposing him to the whole world."

A tingle of alarm shot up his spine. "Cris…"

"I've screenshotted everything and sent emails to all of Clint's contacts and posted all of his conversations online. Let's see how he likes that!"

"I take it the wedding is off?" he asked, giving a rueful look at the package containing the nice tux he just bought for a substantial amount of money.

"Of course the wedding is off! You don't think I'd marry a man like that?"

"You should be careful," he said. "Screenshotting private conversations and then sending them to a person's contacts is probably a crime. He could sue. Better to leave it to the police to go after these people and determine if they've committed a crime."

"I don't care," she said bravely as she sniffed some more. "Monsters like that don't belong in civilized society, Jim. They belong behind bars. And I will not rest until they're all locked up and made to pay for what they did to those poor pets."

Talk about a match made in hell. For a self-professed pet torturer to get engaged to Cristy, who was probably the woman with the biggest heart for pets on the planet must have been one of those tricks fate plays on us, Jim thought. "Just be careful," he told his sister. "And whatever you do, don't go anywhere near the guy. If he finds out what you did, he and his friends might come after you, sis."

"I'm staying with Mom and Dad," she told him.

He smiled. "Of course you are."

No wonder Mom and Dad had never moved Cristy's stuff out of her room. After every failed marriage she moved back home and into her old room.

"I'll drop by later tonight," he promised. "Then you can tell me all about it."

She rang off, and he wondered if he shouldn't go to the police himself. Clearly, Cristy was in such a state that she wouldn't make a lot of sense if she went. They might even think that she was simply a vengeful fiancée who had caught her betrothed in the arms of another woman and was making up stories out of revenge. But then he was reminded of his all-important business meeting and put his sister and her serial bad luck finding a decent husband out of his mind and focused on his presentation. In his line of business, first impressions were everything. And as his success guru didn't mind repeating over and over again, you only had one chance to make a first impression, so better make it count!

And so he went over his sales pitch in his head until he had it nailed down to the last detail, and it was a thing of beauty.

CHAPTER 4

Odelia had been working diligently on her series of articles about the schoolteacher who had been accused of exposing himself indecently to his pupils when her editor knocked on the door of her office and walked in. "Excellent stuff on that Garret Root guy, Odelia," he said as he took a seat in front of her desk. "We need to keep this story hot and on the front page for as long as we can."

"It is a terrible story," she said as she leaned back. "And I don't understand why he hasn't been arrested yet and inter-rogated." She had called her uncle, but he said that Garret Root had vanished from the face of the earth. The moment the accusations had started circulating, he had personally sent a unit to arrest the guy, but they had failed to find him at his home address.

"It's men like Root who give this town a bad name," said the aged editor as he stroked his white beard. "So he's lying low, huh? Maybe hiding out at his parents' place?"

"I don't think so. My uncle dispatched two of his officers to pick the guy up, and I'm sure they thought of paying a visit to his parents and all of his known haunts." She shrugged.

"Looks like he knew something was coming and decided to leave town."

"Skipped out altogether," said Dan. "Cunning. Very cunning." He gave her a keen look. "Now if *we* could track down the guy, that would be quite the scoop, wouldn't you say? Exclusive interview with a wanted man in his lair?"

She smiled. "Are you telling me to go out there and track *down* the guy, Dan?"

"I'm sure I don't even have to tell you. My star reporter will have thought of this all by herself." He got up. "So find me the most wanted man in America and I promise you a nice bonus when you land that exclusive scoop." He tapped his nose. "I've got a hunch that you'll succeed where others have failed."

She watched as he returned to his own office and wondered how to go about finding the guy. Her uncle's officers would have been diligent. They would have paid a visit to all of his relatives, his friends, the school... And if they hadn't found him, where else to look? And it was as she gave herself up to thought that she got a bright idea. From her deep dive into the man's life, she had ascertained that he wasn't married, had no kids of his own, but what he did have was a much-beloved beagle who accompanied him wherever he went—except when he had to work, of course. Though Odelia had talked to one of the guy's colleagues and she had told her that sometimes Garret would bring his dog to school, and the kids loved it. And as she tried to remember the dog's name, she picked up the phone and called her grandmother, who she knew was home babysitting Grace.

* * *

VESTA WAS NOT EXACTLY in a good mood, so when she picked up the phone, it was with a growl. "What do you want!" she practically shouted into the device.

"Someone is feeling grouchy," said her granddaughter.

"Oh, it's just that I never seem to get the cooperation I need."

"As a matter of fact, *I* need your cooperation," said Odelia.

"What is it?"

"I don't know if you've heard, but a teacher is wanted in connection to a crime, and he seems to have gone missing."

"Garret Root," she said, nodding. "I know all about him."

"I've been trying to track him down, but he's disappeared. But then I remembered that he has a dog he takes every-where with him—even to school."

"So?"

"So if we manage to find the dog, we'll be able to find Garret."

"What good would that do? Your uncle will simply let him get away with it again, just like he did before."

"My uncle has been looking everywhere for Garret, but the fact of the matter is that he gave him the slip. So what do you say, Gran? Ask the cats to find the dog?"

She thought for a moment. It's never an easy feat when you've slammed the door on a person to have to come crawling back and ask for their assistance. And since she had just told her cats that she didn't need them, it was tough on her ego to have to admit that she did. But she was nothing if not resourceful, so she knew she'd be able to come up with some excuse. "Consider it done," she said as she glanced through the window to see if Grace was still behaving herself. She shouldn't have worried. The little girl was still on the couch where she was reciting something on her tablet computer while the four cats were fast asleep.

She placed her phone on the table and thought for a moment. And then she got it. She'd simply tell them that the guy wasn't merely an exhibitionist but also liked to torture pets. That should get their attention. And so she got up and returned indoors. Of course, the cats didn't even look up from their slumber.

She loudly cleared her throat. Still no response. So she resorted to the more direct approach by poking Max in the ribs. This time he did open his eyes and gave her a look of annoyance, as if to say: 'What are you up to, silly human person? Can't you see I'm napping?'

"There's been a development," she announced. "That guy I told you about? The schoolteacher who's been exposing his private parts to kids? Turns out he's also been torturing pets."

"Torturing pets?" asked Max, his look of indignation morphing into one of mild interest. "You mean…"

"Do I have to draw you a picture? The guy is a sadist, pure and simple. So we have to stop him before more pets get hurt. And as luck would have it, he has a dog."

"Not so lucky for the dog," said Max.

She saw that she had phrased things a little unfortunately. "According to Odelia, Garret Root owns a dog and if we find the dog, we find the man. So how about it?"

Max yawned. "How about what?"

She rolled her eyes and suppressed a powerful curse. "How about we find the dog, and you talk to the canine and get him to give you his master's whereabouts?"

Max gave her another stare, of the kind that only cats can give. A mixture of 'Get lost' and 'Have we met before?' "Okay," he finally said. "But then who's going to look after Grace?"

"Don't you worry about Grace. We'll take her along with us."

"To look for a known child and pet abuser?"

"We will protect her with our lives."

He shrugged. "It's your call."

Cats. They were impossible.

CHAPTER 5

*D*ooley hadn't really followed the conversation between Gran and Max too closely. All he knew was that Odelia had given them a task to entertain Grace and make sure she didn't get in harm's way. And since he was a conscientious cat in every sense of the word, he took that task very seriously indeed, both the entertainment aspect and the protection part. So when he saw that Grace had jumped off the couch and ventured out of the house through the kitchen door, he decided to tag along and make sure she didn't wander off the property.

Gran was a wonderful human, but if she had a fault—and he wasn't saying she did—it was that she was often distracted by the many projects she got involved with. Like this neighborhood watch thing. Once she had her sights set on a particular person, she hunted him down with a focus that wouldn't have been out of place in a different setting—like if she was an actual serving officer of the law.

"Where are you going?" he asked as he wandered after the little girl.

"I just saw a video about quantum mechanics that says

that time is a relative concept," said Grace. "And so is space. So now I want to test that idea in the real world by doing an experiment."

Dooley was interested in this. Possessing a scientific mind himself, he liked this approach. He was, after all, an avid watcher of the Discovery Channel, which promoted a scientific view of the world and life in general. "What experiment?" he asked, therefore.

"Well, I'm going to climb on top of that chair," she said, indicating the plastic garden chair that Gran had vacated. "And then I'm going to jump off while I think uplifting thoughts. If my calculations are correct, I should end up at the top of that tree over there."

He didn't really follow how one thing would lead to the other, but it was still fascinating to see how the little girl's mind worked. "Or you could climb the tree and end up on the chair," he suggested.

Grace's face lit up into a smile. "I like your thinking, Dooley. So why don't you climb that tree, and I'll climb the chair, and let's see if we don't end up switching places!"

It sure sounded like an interesting experiment, and so he eagerly subscribed to be Grace's assistant in testing out the quantum mechanic approach to climbing trees and garden chairs. It didn't take him all that long to reach the top of the tree, since he had the benefit of sharp claws to sustain his ascent. And as he looked down, he saw that Grace had indeed managed to climb that chair.

"Now, Dooley!" she yelled. "Think uplifting thoughts!"

And so he closed his eyes and thought of his good friend Max, and what a blessing it was to have him in his life. He also thought of his humans, who were all such lovely and wonderful people. But most of all, he thought of Grace and what an honor it was that she would have picked him as her assistant. Already he could see her as an adult person, teaching at the university, with him by her side to help her explain certain topics to her students. Now, wouldn't that be fun!

"Open your eyes!" she yelled. But when he did as she said, he saw that he was still at the top of that tree, and she was still on top of that chair, and neither of them had moved an inch.

Grace scratched her head. "I think we made a mistake somewhere," she said. "Let me think what it could be." But then she snapped her fingers. "Oh, I've got it. Silly me. We shouldn't merely think uplifting thoughts, but also picture ourselves in our new respective locations. Close your eyes again, Dooley."

He did as he was told.

"Now visualize yourself on a garden chair. Think garden chair!"

So he thought garden chair and put every ounce of imagination into that chair. He saw the chair, he felt the chair, he could even taste the chair!

"Open your eyes!" she instructed.

Once again, he wasn't anywhere near the chair, but when he looked down, he saw that Grace wasn't in the chair either!

"It worked!" he cried, excitement making him giddy. "It really worked!"

"No, it didn't," Grace's voice sounded. When he searched around for her new location, he saw that she wasn't in the tree, as he had surmised, but still on terra firma, though now standing underneath the tree looking up at him.

"But you moved," he said.

"Because I jumped off the chair," she explained. She gave him a bright smile. "Okay, so now all I have to do is climb this tree, and you have to climb down and mount that chair, and then our experiment will have succeeded one way or another." She held up a very professorial finger. "No matter whether the cat is white or black, as long as it catches mice, it is a good cat. Chairman Mao. Now jump, Dooley—jump!"

The last thing he wanted to do was jump, but he also didn't want to ruin Grace's experiment, which seemed to be very important for her and her future career as a college professor. But in the end, try as he might, he couldn't find the courage to take that leap. He also didn't understand that gag about a white cat and a black cat. So as he admitted defeat, he gave her a sad look. "I'm scared."

"Don't be scared," she said. "Quantum mechanics teaches us that time and space don't exist. So nothing will happen to you if you jump—nothing at all. Just think like a bird, Dooley. Think like a tweetie bird. And you'll simply fly away!"

She was probably right, but even as he thought as much like a bird as he could, he sprouted no wings, and he had to accept that he might think he was a bird until the cows came home, but he would never be one. Which is when he started mewling piteously, hoping someone would save him from his predicament!

CHAPTER 6

Tressa O'Keefe had been working hard all morning and felt that she deserved a break. So she leaned back in her chair and addressed her co-worker Bonnie Gallacher. "Wanna grab a coffee and a blueberry muffin?"

Bonnie grimaced and responded without taking her eyes off her computer screen or her fingers off the keyboard. "Yes to the coffee, no to the muffin."

"Counting calories again, huh?"

"That's right. Need to get fit for this wedding I've got coming up. I'm one of the bridesmaids and I don't want to look like a sausage compared to the stick insects."

"That bad?"

"Worse. The bride is probably the most gorgeous woman you've ever seen—she could model for Victoria's Secret and I'm not even kidding. And the other bridesmaids are all fellow models who look as if they've walked straight off the runway. So the only one who'll stick out is me—and not in a good way either!"

"Don't be too hard on yourself, Bonnie," said Tressa. "You look fine to me."

Bonnie gave her a 'Are you kidding me?' look. "I don't look fine, Tressa. I look like a whale. I didn't even fit into the dress Cristy had picked out for me, in spite of the fact that we all had to post our measurements. Talk about humiliation."

"When is the wedding?"

"This weekend. Which gives me exactly..." She thought for a moment. "Three days and twelve hours to get slim. Should be doable, right?"

"Absolutely," said Tressa, who had been in the same situation when her sister got married. She also had the body of a supermodel and next to her Tressa looked like a slob. But she hadn't let it bother her then and she was determined not to let it bother Bonnie now. As the oldest employee of Lexie Twigg Syndication, which handled the rights to about a dozen of the most popular newspaper comic strips in the country, she had often felt that she was like a mother hen to all of these youngsters. And she felt especially protective of Bonnie, in whom she recognized a lot of herself at that age.

"The thing is..." Bonnie hesitated and bit her lip as she glanced around to see if any of the other twenty or so employees who worked for the syndicate were listening.

"What is it?"

"Well, I got a mysterious message from Cristy this morning, so now I'm wondering if the wedding might be postponed."

"What did she write?"

Bonnie picked up her phone. "'Men are the scum of the earth. Respond if you agree. Unfriend me if you don't.' Of course I agreed since I don't want her to unfriend me. But it got me thinking that maybe, just maybe, there might be trouble in paradise."

"I think there's a pretty good chance there is. So maybe there won't be a wedding?"

"After all the trouble we all went to, that would be such a shame. And also, Cristy's fiancé Clint is such a catch. Easily the most handsome guy I've ever met. Not only easy on the eyes but also very nice." She laughed. "In fact, if Cristy doesn't want him, I might go after the guy myself!"

Tressa smiled. Her young colleague's love life was probably one of the most discussed topics at the office—or she should probably say: her lack of a love life. It was true that Bonnie's measurements were on the generous side, but she made up for that with a sunny disposition and a big heart. Any man should count himself lucky to have her. But unfortunately, she hadn't had a lot of luck in that department, with date after date turning into a disaster, the excruciating details of which she then regaled her colleagues with, much to the hilarity of all.

"Maybe you should call Cristy and ask her what's going on," Tressa advised now. "Before you go and starve yourself to death for a wedding that won't even happen."

"Yeah, I guess you're right," said Bonnie. She glanced around for Candace, their supervisor, and when she saw she wasn't at her desk, she dropped her voice to a conspiratorial whisper. "So maybe we'll have that coffee break now?"

"Yeah, let's," said Tressa. Even though it wasn't strictly break time yet, she felt they had earned a respite from the piles of work on their respective desks. She didn't know what was going on, but lately their workload had easily doubled, and sometimes even tripled, with no end in sight. As far as she could ascertain, the syndicate had taken on a batch of new accounts but hadn't hired new people to handle the increase in work—effectively saving money on staff.

She got up from behind her desk, grabbed her purse, and the two friends and colleagues were off. Taking the elevator, they soon arrived in the giant glass atrium of the building where the syndicate shared office space with similar businesses, and walked out of the front door en route to their favorite coffee shop, located around the corner. As they walked over, Bonnie told her a few more details about her good friend Cristy, namely the fact that she had been married before, and none of her previous marriages had lasted longer than a couple of years, with one even collapsing in a matter of days, after Cristy discovered that her new husband had slept with one of her bridesmaids.

"I was really hoping that this time things would work out," she confessed. "She's the nicest person in the world, and one of my oldest friends, and if anyone deserves everlasting love and happiness, it's Cristy."

They had arrived at the Happy Bean and walked in to find the place buzzing, in spite of the early hour. They both stepped up to the counter to order their regular, and Tressa saw that the same barista was standing at attention for the growing line of clientele. He was tall and handsome with a square jaw and a three-day stubble, and when he smiled, it made her heart beat a little faster—or a lot.

She didn't like to admit it, but he was one of the main reasons she preferred to frequent this particular coffee shop above any of the other, cheaper, and possibly better ones in the area.

"Hi, Douglas," she said coyly when it was finally their turn.

"Ladies!" he said with a wide smile. "What can I do for you today?"

"Oh, just the regular," said Bonnie. "But if you can add some extra foam, that would be very welcome."

"Extra foam it is," he said. "And what about you, Tressa? Same as usual?"

She nodded gratefully, surprised that he would have remembered her name. "Thanks, Douglas."

"Order is coming right up," he said.

They proceeded to their table by the window, and she noticed that Bonnie was giving her a strange look. "Is there something going on between you and Douglas that I should know about?" she asked.

"Oh, don't be silly," said Tressa. "I'm old enough to be his mother."

"All the same. Some men are attracted to older women, just like some women are attracted to younger guys." She leaned in and touched Tressa's arm. "He seems like a great guy. So why don't you ask for his number?"

"*Me* ask for *his* number? No way," she said, both exhilarated at the prospect and horrified.

"Long gone are the days that men have to take the initiative," said Bonnie. "If you like Douglas, you should let him know. He might like you, too."

"Nuh-uh," she said, but she couldn't hide the fact that her cheeks were coloring, and her heart was racing at the prospect of asking the handsome barista out on a date. She darted a furtive look in his direction, and as luck would have it, she met his eyes, and if she wasn't mistaken, there was definite interest reflected in them. But then she quickly discarded the thought. Men like Douglas weren't interested in women like her. And besides, he probably had a girlfriend.

"You really should put yourself out there again, Tressa," Bonnie insisted. "How long has it been now? Two years? Three?"

"Three and a half," she said.

"That's a long time to be alone. Too long, if you ask me."

The story of Tressa's own love life was an open book at the office, with pretty much everyone knowing by now that her husband had died when the couple were on vacation in Thailand. Robert had been taking a selfie and had ventured too close to the edge of a cliff and had promptly fallen to his death. And since Tressa had been at the hotel at the time, it had been hours before his body was discovered, and the terrible news relayed to her. They'd been married for twenty years, and suddenly it was all over. At least they'd never had kids, which was both a part of her own personal tragedy and, in hindsight, perhaps a blessing, since their kids would never have to miss their father or go through the pain Tressa had gone through.

She gave her friend a smile. Looks like the roles were suddenly reversed, with Bonnie giving her advice on her love life and not the other way around.

"What?" asked Bonnie. "He's hot. And if you don't go after him, maybe I will."

"Be my guest," she said. "But I gotta tell you that he looks like a player."

Bonnie shrugged. "So? Maybe I like to be played with once in a while. Don't you?"

She laughed out loud. "Yeah, I guess I do."

Their drinks arrived, and when she picked up her double vanilla cinnamon latte with nutmeg on top, she saw that something was written on the side.

It was a telephone number, and if she wasn't mistaken, it was Douglas's.

CHAPTER 7

When we stepped out of the house to go in search of this illustrious beagle, we came upon a heart-wrenching scene: Dooley was in the top of the big tree, and Grace was at the bottom of it, encouraging him to 'think like a bird.' But obviously that wasn't working too well for him, since try as he might, he didn't seem to be able to sprout wings on command and fly down out of that tree.

"Dooley, what are you doing up there?" Gran demanded.

"We're trying a quantum mechanic experiment," Dooley announced. "But so far it isn't working out the way we hoped."

"Just get down from there, will you?" said Gran. "We have to go and see a dog about a man."

"I want to come down," Dooley announced. "But I don't seem to be able to."

He was absolutely right, of course, and had touched upon one of the only flaws I've ever been able to detect in the feline species, which otherwise is perfect to a degree: we don't possess a reverse gear. And so when we climb a tree, we can't back down the way a human would. Instead, we have to proceed down headfirst, which is not a course of action I would advise, since it can only lead to disaster.

"I think you'll have to go and get him, Gran," Brutus now said.

"Me? Go up there? No way!" said Gran.

"It's the only way," Harriet pointed out.

"And break my neck?"

"You could use Tex's ladder," I suggested.

Odelia's dad has a very nice ladder just for these circumstances. Though in actual fact, he probably uses it for other stuff as well.

"I'm not going up there," said Gran. "I may be a lot of things, but I'm not suicidal." But she wasn't blind to the predicament our friend was in, and I could tell that she was already working on a possible solution. "I'll just have to phone Chase," she said. "He's got experience with this kind of thing, after all."

The smiles that appeared on all of our faces were a testament to this: each time one of us has gotten stuck in a tree in the past, Chase has always been there to save us. So hopefully, he would be able to find time in his busy schedule to save Dooley.

Moments later, Gran was in communication with Odelia's husband and was explaining to him the ins and outs of the situation. But apparently, she didn't like what he was telling her, if her frown was any indication. "What do you mean you're busy on a case? What could be more important than saving one of your cats?" She listened for a few moments more, then uttered a few words I won't repeat and promptly hung up on the cop. "I think it's time that Odelia starts looking for a new husband," she told us. "This one is obviously not as invested in this family as I thought he was. If he can't even take the short drive over here to do this little thing…" She tapped her bottom lip with her phone, then her face brightened. "Oh, I know. I'll ask Alec. I'm sure he's got nothing else to do." And so before long, she was calling the chief of police. But when he informed her that he was busy too, it was all she could do not to throw her phone into the bushes and give up on her relatives, none of whom seemed to be prepared to drop everything and come to our assistance.

"Maybe you could ask the fire department," I suggested. "They have helped us out before."

"I guess so," she said. "Though why call the fire department when you've got perfectly capable male members of your family who could assist—if only they'd be bothered to." But in the end, she saw no other recourse but to call 911. But before she could form the number, suddenly a man showed up in our backyard. For a moment, he merely looked around, as if uncertain how to proceed. I saw that he was accompanied by a dog of the beagle variety, who looked just about as out of place as the man seemed to be.

"And what do *you* want?" Gran growled, in her usual irascible tone.

"Um... is this the home of Odelia Kingsley?" asked the man. "The reporter?"

"Who wants to know?" asked Gran suspiciously.

"Are you Odelia Kingsley?" asked the man.

"Do I look like Odelia Kingsley?" Gran shot back.

The man hesitated. "I'm not sure," he ventured. "You see, I've never met Mrs. Kingsley, so I don't know what she looks like."

"Oh, for crying out loud," said Gran. "Can't you see I'm busy?" She gestured to Dooley, who had resorted to quietly mewling from the top of the tree, and holding on for dear life all the while.

"Is that cat stuck up there?" asked the man.

"No, he's pretending to be a Christmas star—of course he's stuck up there! And since none of my family members

33

can be bothered to help him down from there, I will have to call the fire department. And you know they'll give me a lot of grief and accuse me of being negligent."

"If you like, I could get him down from there," the man suggested.

We all shared a look of surprise. It isn't every day that a stranger suddenly turns up on your doorstep and offers his kind assistance in a matter of the greatest urgency. For if Dooley stayed up there for half an hour longer, he might get seriously traumatized.

Gran eyed the man curiously. "You'd be willing to do that for me?"

"Well, of course, Mrs. Kingsley," said the man. "But only if I can state my case to you."

Gran shrugged. "Okay, be my guest. Get my cat down from that tree, and then we'll talk."

And so he spat on his hands, and moments later was climbing that tree as if he had never done anything else his entire life. We all watched on with bated breath as he took on this daring task, and as he steadily climbed up, I said, "Gran, you probably should have told him that you're not Odelia."

"And risk him pulling out of saving Dooley? No way, José."

"But you will tell him when he gets down from there, won't you?"

"Providing he doesn't break his neck? Sure."

The man had now reached the top rung of the tree and reached out an inviting hand to Dooley. "Here, kitty, kitty," he said.

"Max, there's a weird man trying to snatch me!" Dooley cried. "Do I scratch him?"

"Do not scratch him, Dooley," I said. "I repeat: do not scratch that man. He's only trying to get you down from there."

"Oh, so his intentions are good?"

"They are—absolutely," I assured our friend.

Greatly reassured by this, Dooley allowed the man to grab him and tuck him inside his jacket, and then start to make his way down again.

"I've got to hand it to him," said Gran with a look of admiration on her face. "He's got the technique down pat. Looks like he's done this kind of thing before."

"Maybe he's a fireman," Harriet suggested.

"Yeah, he does have a great technique," Brutus agreed.

Before long, the man stood with both feet back on solid ground, and as he released Dooley from his jacket, our beloved friend sighed with relief. "Oh, what an adventure! What a thrill! Though next time, I don't think I'll trust quantum mechanics to get me out of a tree anymore!"

"You probably didn't try hard enough," said Grace, the harsh taskmaster.

The guy dusted off his hands. "So can we talk now, Mrs. Kingsley?"

For a moment, Gran didn't respond. Then a sly smile spread across her face. "Sure thing, bud. Tell me all about it."

CHAPTER 8

"The thing is, Mrs. Kingsley," said the man, "that I find myself in something of a pickle—the nature of which I cannot even begin to understand. So I read online that you take on the occasional case, and since I'm all out of options here, I thought I'd ask you if you could look into this particular problem I'm facing."

"And what is your problem?" asked Gran.

She had invited Dooley's savior to take a seat on one of the plastic garden chairs Odelia and Chase had purchased. He still hadn't cottoned on to the fact that she wasn't the actual Odelia Kingsley but her grandmother, though the fact that he hadn't been offered a refreshment yet should have given him a clue. Odelia is nothing if not the perfect hostess, and she always offers her guests refreshments.

The man took a deep breath. "I should probably start by introducing myself. My name is Garret Root, and I'm a schoolteacher at the Gordon Jovitt School."

Gran gasped, and so, I think, did the rest of us. She had set out to find Garret Root, the most wanted and most hated man in America, and here Garret Root had walked straight into our backyard. What were the odds?

"Did you say something?" asked Garret.

But Gran pressed her lips together and shook her head. "No," she finally managed. "Please continue, Mr. Root."

"Call me Garret," he said. "So the thing I don't understand is this," he said, and retrieved a newspaper from his jacket pocket and smoothed it out on the table. "This is me," he said, pointing to the front page. "Though for the life of me I don't understand what they're referring to."

"'SICK PERVERT CAUGHT IN THE ACT!'" Gran read. "'Garret Root—Most Hated Man In America?'" She glanced up at the man. "It's not rocket science, Garret. It says right here that you're a pervert. So what don't you understand?"

"Because I'm not! I never exposed myself to any of the kids. I'm a respected teacher—teacher of the year five years in a row, in fact. The kids love me."

"And you love the kids—a little too much, if this article is to be believed."

"Well, that's exactly it. It's all a pack of lies. I never exposed any part of my anatomy to anyone, and I don't understand where this paper gets its information."

"There must be some truth to it," Gran argued. "Or why else would they print it? And on the front page, no less. Prime newspaper real estate, Garret. A lot of people would fight to have their picture printed above the fold."

"Well, not me, all right?" he said with a touch of belligerence. "I never did any of the stuff they're accusing me of, and I would like you to look into this and find out what's going on."

Gran had picked up her phone and was scrolling through a litany of other news articles. "They're all saying the same thing, Garret," she said as she held up the phone. "Most wanted man. Most hated man. Most despised man. Pervert of the year. Why would they all lie about this?"

"I don't know!" he said, flapping his arms a little. "But I swear to you that I didn't do this, Mrs. Kingsley. I'm innocent."

"Like the driven snow, no doubt," she said skeptically. "Look, Garret. The best advice I can give you right now is to turn yourself in. If you're really innocent, and these allegations are a pack of lies, the investigation will get to the bottom of it. My son—I mean, my uncle is the chief of police, and he's very good at what he does. So if you tell him what you've just told me, I can promise that he will take a good long look at these allegations and get to the truth of what's being said about you. But if you stay on the run, like you have been, it won't end well for you."

"I haven't been on the run," he said, looking crestfallen all of a sudden. "I only found out about this an hour ago when people in the street started yelling bad things at me."

"So where have you been all this time? The police have been looking for you."

"I was upstate visiting a friend. We went hiking in the mountains, and I just arrived back this morning." He gestured to the paper. "Only to find that in my absence, suddenly I've become America's most hated and most wanted man."

"That must have come as quite a shock to you," I told the beagle, eager to make the dog's acquaintance and find out what it thought about this whole business.

"Oh, it *was* a big shock," the beagle agreed. "I even had a dog come up to me in the street this morning and tell me I should find a new owner, since my current one will be in prison before nightfall and will probably be old and gray by the time he gets out again." He shook his head. "Talk about a pleasant homecoming."

"So what's your name?" asked Harriet kindly. We may be cats, but that doesn't mean we have to be mean to dogs. After all, they are companion animals, just like us.

"Susan," said the dog.

We all stared at him. "But... you are a male dog, aren't you?" asked Brutus.

"Yeah, I guess there was a mix-up when I was born," said the dog. "Garret was told I was a female, so he called me Susan. And then later the vet told him I wasn't a female, but since we'd both gotten used to the name, he decided to stick with it."

"Okay, Susan," said Harriet, "so what can you tell us about Garret? Did he really do the things they're accusing him of in the paper?"

"And does he torture pets?" Brutus added.

"I'm not my human's keeper," said Susan carefully, prefacing his remarks with a caveat as any good lawyer would, "and we're not together twenty-four hours, so I don't know what he does when I'm not with him, but that being said..." He took a deep breath. "I don't recognize the man they're describing in those articles as Garret. I mean, the Garret I know is a kindhearted and good man who would never do any of the things they're accusing him of. And he certainly has never tortured me."

"So he wouldn't have exposed himself to any of those kids?" I asked.

Susan shook his head. "Not the Garret I know. But like I said, we're not joined at the hip, so I can't rule out that he did something that could be interpreted as inappropriate. But if he says he's innocent, I for one am inclined to believe him."

"Well, that's good enough for us," said Brutus. He turned to me. "Isn't that right, Max?"

I wasn't prepared to go there yet, so instead, I decided to

ask a couple of follow-up questions. "Have there been any complaints about him in the past, that you know of?"

"Never," said Susan determinedly.

"Any parents questioning his behavior around their kids?"

"Nothing of the kind."

"Has Garret ever been called into the principal's office?"

"Not even once. He's a model teacher and an ambassador of the school."

I exchanged a look with Gran and shook my head. Gran shrugged. I could tell that she was of the opinion that dogs aren't exactly the best character witnesses, seeing as they've got a reputation for remaining loyal to their humans, no matter what. And I guess she has a point. I mean, even notorious gangsters have owned dogs, and I very much doubt if they would have disowned their humans.

Still, Susan's steadfast but nuanced denial of any wrongdoing on the part of Garret made me question the accuracy of the news reports. Which begged the question of where those stories had originated. Who had filed that complaint? And if Garret truly was innocent, then what exactly was going on here?

"Okay, let's get down to the nitty-gritty," said Gran. "Who is accusing you and why?" She had picked up the paper again. "The accuser's name is being withheld, but the paper does quote one of your colleagues." She frowned at the paper. "One Melody Jarram? And she has a lot of very bad things to say about you, Garret. I even get the impression that she may have filed the original complaint."

He sighed. "Melody has been in love with me for years, but because I never felt the same way about her, I was forced to go to the principal at one point and ask her to talk to Melody, since she wouldn't listen to me. The principal did talk to her, and Melody has never forgiven me. It isn't too much to say that her affection turned to hatred."

"So what are you saying? That this Melody made up these accusations?"

"It's possible," he said. "I actually tried contacting her after I read the article, but she's blocking my calls. So frankly, I don't know what's going on."

"Did you talk to your principal?"

"I did, and she told me not to come in today, or any day for the near future. I'm suspended while they investigate the claims that have been made against me."

"Gotcha." She thought for a moment, then glanced down at me. I gave her a shrug, indicating I thought this case might be worth pursuing. "Okay, Garret," she said finally. "I'm going to take on your case. But only on one condition."

The man looked extremely relieved. "And what's that?"

"You have to promise me to turn yourself in."

He was shaking his head before she had finished the sentence. "I can't."

She gave him a penetrating look. "You have no other choice. I'll go with you, but you have to stop running. Like I said, Alec is a good cop. He won't charge you simply based on some rumors from a disgruntled colleague."

"It's not that," said Garret as he gave Gran a pained look. "It's my sister."

"Your sister? What's she got to do with this?"

"She's getting married this weekend, and she'll never forgive me if I stand her up. So let me attend the wedding and then I'll turn myself in—I promise."

Gran frowned. "Don't you think your sister would prefer if you didn't attend her wedding? I mean, no offense, but if I were getting married and my brother was wanted by the police, I'd tell him to stay as far away from me as possible."

He rubbed his chin. "I hadn't thought about it like that."

"My advice? Give your sister a break and go to the police

now. And in the meantime, I'll look into your case and get to the bottom of what is going on."

He nodded, but I could see from the mulish look that had come into his eyes that Gran's advice didn't sit well with him at all. Clearly, this wedding was important to him, and he wouldn't miss it for the world—even if that world wanted him badly for a crime he claimed he did not commit.

"Okay," he said finally. "I'll turn myself in."

Gran relaxed. "Good man. Wait here while I go and get my purse. We'll go together, so I can explain to my son—my uncle, I mean—what you just told me."

She got up and walked into the house. For a few beats, Garret just sat there, then all of a sudden, he sprang up from his chair and walked off.

"Susan, come," he said curtly.

Susan rolled his eyes. "Here we go," she said. "On the run again."

"You don't have to follow him," I told the beagle.

He gave me a lopsided grin. "I'm a dog, Max. What am I going to do? Abandon my master? You know as well as I do that goes against the dog's code."

I guess he had a point.

And so we watched Garret and Susan hurry off around the side of the building. When Gran returned moments later, she seemed perturbed to find that the would-be criminal had disappeared.

"Where did he go?" she asked.

"I guess he really wants to attend that wedding," I said.

Gran allowed herself to sink back into her chair. "Oh, you stupid, stupid man," she said quietly. Then she resigned herself to the circumstances. "Oh, well. It's his funeral."

"You are going to take on his case, aren't you, Gran?" asked Dooley.

"Of course I'm going to take on his case," she said. "Only

by the time I get to the bottom of it, he'll probably be in jail—and being a fugitive from justice won't do him much good. And neither will his sister be thrilled when he's arrested in front of her wedding guests and just before she's had a chance to say, 'I do.'"

CHAPTER 9

*J*im had parked his car in the underground parking garage located beneath the Star Hotel and was just about to take the elevator up to the lobby when a man accosted him. At first, he didn't recognize the man, as he chose to remain in the shadows, but when he spoke, he realized that it was none other than his brother!

"Garret!" he said. "What are you doing here?"

"I'm in trouble, Jim," said Garret, finally stepping out of the shadows. "I need a place to lay low for a couple of days. Can I stay at yours?"

"Of course," said Jim. "But what's going on?"

Garret gave him a strange look. "I take it you haven't read the news?"

"I've been busy," said Jim. He gestured to the elevator. "I'm trying to land the biggest deal of my career, and if I pull this off, I'm on velvet. If not…"

"My advice? Don't read the news," said Garret.

"But why?"

"They're trying to frame me for something I didn't do.

44

And I swear to God that's the God's honest truth." Garret's dog Susan barked once, as if to confirm this statement.

"What exactly are they accusing you of?" asked Jim, starting to become more than a little worried now.

"It's not important," said Garret. "Just promise that if the police ask you about it, you haven't seen me, all right?"

"The police? Why would the police..." His worry increased with leaps and bounds. "What did you do, Garret?"

His brother hemmed and hawed for a moment, then finally came clean. "They're accusing me of being an exhibitionist."

"Oh, my God!"

"But it's all lies!"

"Who's accusing you?"

"The victim's identity is being withheld, so I have no idea who's behind this whole thing. All I know is that I took off on my hiking trip on Friday and when I came back it was all over the papers that I'm some kind of monster or something."

"Did you talk to the police?"

"What good would that do? They'd just lock me up and throw away the key. No, I have to fight this on my own, Jim."

"Did you hire a lawyer?"

"I did something much better than that. I engaged Odelia Kingsley."

"The reporter?"

"She's also an amateur sleuth. And she promised to take on my case."

"Well, at least that's something," said Jim, as he ran a hand through his hair. "Look, I've got to run," he said. "I can't be late for this meeting. But make yourself comfortable at home, and I'll see you later tonight, all right? We can talk about this thing and really thresh it out. Though I would still advise you to talk to a lawyer. The Kingsley woman may be good, but she's not a lawyer. And once the police get a hold of you, you will want someone next to you to advise you of your rights."

"Thanks, little brother," said Garret, giving him a look of relief. "I won't forget this."

"Just make sure that nobody sees you entering the house," he advised. "Knowing my neighbors, they're liable to call the cops the moment they see your face."

He watched as Garret retreated back into the shadows. Moments later, a car's engine was fired up, and the little green Toyota Garret drove made its way to the exit. He shook his head. Between Cristy's wedding—or non-wedding as it now looked increasingly likely—and Garret's problems with the law, it would appear as if these next couple of days might prove to be extremely eventful.

But then he pulled himself together. He had a business meeting to attend, and he couldn't let his mind wander to all kinds of dark places. So he told himself to focus on the meeting to the exclusion of everything else. Which he soon discovered was easier said than done, for his mind kept flashing back to both Garret and Cristy's stories.

* * *

As GARRET DROVE his car in the direction of his brother's place, Susan kept giving him what he could only interpret as accusing glances. "Why are you looking at me like that?" he asked finally.

The dog gave a soft woofle.

"Look, I had to get away from there," he explained. "The Kingsley woman was going to turn me in to the cops, and the last thing I need right now is to languish in some jail somewhere with no access to any of my resources."

It might be just his imagination, but Susan actually shook his head in abject dismay at his poor choices.

"I didn't do this, all right?" he cried.

Even his own dog seemed to accuse him. At least Jim was in his corner. The one conversation he dreaded more than most was with his sister Cristy. The last thing he wanted was to spoil her wedding. Now that she had finally found a man she could be happy with, she didn't need his legal problems to interfere with that.

He arrived at Jim's place and parked in front of the house. He glanced left and right before he got out, remembering his brother's warning not to allow himself to be seen by the neighbors. When he thought the coast was clear, he got out, locked the car, and jogged over to the house. Good thing he had a key to the place, as he also had a key to Cristy's apartment, and his brother and sister had keys to his apartment as well. They were a tight-knit family in that sense.

He inserted his key in the lock and let himself and Susan in. The moment the door closed, he breathed a sigh of relief. Here he could lie down for the time being without being harassed by strangers in the street about his alleged wrongdoings or being pressured into going to the police.

He then took out his phone and pulled up Cristy's number. On the drive over, he had finally decided on the course of action he would pursue. And so when his sister's voice sounded in his ear, he put on his most cheerful voice.

"Hey, sis. I don't know if you've read the news..."

"What news? Is it Clint? Has he called you about the wedding?"

"Clint? No, I didn't hear from Clint."

"Good. If he does, don't pick up. In fact, simply block his number on your phone right now."

His mood sank as quickly as a stone. "Why?"

"Because he's a low-life piece of pond scum, that's why!"

He closed his eyes. "Don't tell me. The wedding is off?"

"Of course the wedding is off. I'm not going to marry a man who gets off on torturing innocent pets. In fact, I'm at the police station right now to file an official complaint against that horrible man and the rest of his gang of sickos." She paused for a moment. "So what was it that you wanted to tell me?"

"Oh, nothing," he said. "Just that I'm staying at Jim's for the time being. So if you need me, you know where to find me." But then he realized he probably shouldn't have said that. "You're at the police station?"

"That's right. Waiting for my interview. Why?"

"Forget I said that I'm at Jim's."

"Why? What's going on, Garret?"

He hesitated for a moment, then decided to tell her the whole story. Her response wasn't as emotional as he had expected, but then if she was in the police station waiting room, she probably had to watch what she said.

"I don't believe this," she said. "My own brother, accused of…" She didn't say the words out loud, which was probably a good thing, for he was sick and tired of hearing it by now. "Look, I'll finish up my business here and then I'll drive straight over, and we can talk about this. First thing we need to do is to get you a good lawyer. And the second thing…" There was a noise on the other end, and she suddenly whispered, "I'm going in—wish me luck!"

And then she was gone. He just hoped she wouldn't tell the cops all about where he was laying low. Knowing his sister, she just might blab it all out!

CHAPTER 10

It was with some reluctance that we set out to assist Gran in her quest to either condemn or exonerate Garret Root, depending on what we would find. Reluctant because I'd much rather finish that pleasant nap I'd been enjoying, but also with a sense of responsibility since Susan had personally asked us to put our best paw forward to see that justice was done.

"I have a hunch that he didn't do it," said Gran as we all piled into the little red Peugeot she likes to use for neighborhood watch purposes. "And I'll tell you why. The guy has an honest face. And a face like that can't possibly be guilty of the crime they're accusing him of."

"So you think he's innocent because you like his face, Gran?" asked Dooley.

"That's exactly right. And let me tell you something else," she said as she poked at the ignition until her key fit and then jammed it in. "As possibly the greatest judge of character that has ever lived, my hunches are never wrong."

"So why are we going out there at all?" asked Harriet, who

suppressed a yawn. "If your hunch tells you the guy is innocent, we might just as well stay home."

"We still gotta prove it, Harriet," said Gran as she caused the engine to whine in protest at the harsh treatment she was subjecting it to. "And not only to the cops but to the whole world. So we need some solid evidence that the guy is being framed. Which means we have to find the person responsible, and that's going to require some good old-fashioned detective work." She turned to the four of us, hunched up on the backseat, like astronauts strapped in for the moment that big rocket hurls them into space. "So are you ready to go and do some sleuthing?"

"Yes, Gran," we said in unison, more because her voice brooked no contest than out of sheer conviction or excitement about the prospect of going on a wild goose chase with the oldest member of our human household.

"Then let's go!" she said, and stomped her foot down on the accelerator.

The car emitted a sound of surprise, then bucked and jumped around for a moment, before peeling away from the curb and almost hitting a milk truck that came from the other direction. For some reason, Gran seems to think that a car only has two modes of operation: full throttle or idling at the curb. There's simply no middle ground. But then I guess that describes her general view of life.

"First, we'll pick up Scarlett," she announced. "Since a good detective needs to have a sidekick. And then we'll drop by that school and talk to this Melody Jarram woman and put her on the hot seat." A grim-faced look came over her as she gripped her steering wheel until her knuckles went white. "I'll make her sing like a canary, just you wait and see!"

We shared a look of concern. "Do you think she will torture Mrs. Jarram?" asked Brutus.

"I have a feeling she will," said Harriet.

"But isn't that illegal?" asked Dooley.

"Gran feels she's above the law," I said. "So in that sense, Mrs. Jarram won't know what hit her." Which maybe was a good thing if she really was responsible for spreading these ugly rumors about the man she once professed to love.

It wasn't long before Gran jerked the car to a stop in front of Scarlett Canyon's apartment block, causing us to fall from the backseat and end up in the footwell, which wasn't a pleasant sensation. By the time we had disentangled our limbs and made sure none had gone missing, Gran had already exited the vehicle and was pounding up the walkway to her friend's edifice.

"Maybe Odelia shouldn't have asked her grandmother to assist her in this investigation," said Harriet, voicing a thought we were all thinking. "Her style doesn't exactly lend itself to the subtle approach a case like this requires."

"Yeah, Odelia should have taken the case in hand personally," I agreed wholeheartedly.

"Gran will get us all thrown in the slammer," said Brutus with a shiver. "And we all know what that means: rats!"

As we gave ourselves up to visions of a rat-infested jail cell, I swore a solemn oath to make sure that didn't happen. And so I vowed to prove or disprove Garret Root's innocence the first chance I got, so that Gran wouldn't have to.

As we watched through the car window, we saw her return with her friend Scarlett in tow. The two old ladies were talking animatedly as Gran explained to her the ins and outs of the case that had been dropped in their laps.

Scarlett got in and installed herself in the passenger seat before turning and giving us a cheerful wave. "Oh, you guys, I'm so excited! Finally a real case to sink our teeth into. Aren't you excited?"

"Oh, we're very excited," said Brutus with a voice as if rising from the tomb.

"Especially about the rats," Harriet added in an equally cheerless voice.

"It won't come to that," I told my friends. "And to make sure it doesn't, we'll have to take this case in paw like we've never done before. And to that end, we'll have to collaborate. We'll have to coordinate. And we'll have to cooperate."

"That's a lot of 'ating,' Max," said Brutus. "Are we sure we'll be able to pull it off?"

"We'll have to," I said simply. "Unless you want to have this whole thing go off the rails in a spectacular fashion?"

My three friends all shook their heads, and so it was decided: regardless of what Gran was up to, or how she chose to conduct herself in the coming hours, days, and weeks, we'd launch a parallel investigation of our own, and make sure we were successful. Our safety, sanity, and general well-being depended on it!

CHAPTER 11

Odelia walked into her husband's office after a brief knock on the door and saw that Chase was busy on the phone. When he became aware of her presence, he held up his finger in an indication that his call would only take another minute, so she let herself sink down into the armchair the cop had placed in the corner of his office and glanced out the window. The armchair had been a gift from the mother of one of Chase's colleagues, who was doing a yard sale and had been left stuck with this particular armchair that nobody seemed to want. It was an old specimen that had been in the family for years and probably was better suited for a landfill than the office of Hampton Cove's premier detective. But then Chase claimed that it helped him think when he was tackling a particularly tough case, so the armchair had been saved from a bad fate and had found a second home.

The field behind the police office was a wild tangle of weeds and bushes, and rumor had it that a family of rats lived there. Once upon a time, it was going to be turned into a parking lot, but budget constraints and a lack of initiative had forestalled such a development for now. She thought for a moment about her grandmother's message that she and the cats were on the case of the falsely accused Garret Root, and she didn't really know what to think of all of that. On the one hand, she sincerely wished that the man was indeed innocent of the crime he was being accused of, but on the other hand...

Someone had filed a complaint, so logic dictated that there was a victim and also a perpetrator. And if Garret wasn't the perp, someone else was.

Chase finally ended his call and gave her his full attention. "I know what you're going to say, and I'm on it," he announced before she had a chance to open her mouth.

She raised an eyebrow. "Are you psychic now? Or is this what happens when a couple has been married for a while? They start to read each other's minds?"

"She was in here just now," said Chase. "And I've already started looking into the guy." He glanced down at his notes. "Clint Bearman, right? And I agree that it is a crime that shouldn't go unpunished. And so I've told your uncle that I'll personally handle it." He gave her a proud look, but when she returned his look with a look of bewilderment, his smile slipped from his face. "You're not here about the pet torture club?"

She stared at her hubby. "Pet torture club? Is there a pet torture club?"

"There is. Or at least if..." Once again, he glanced down at his notes. "Cristy Root is to be believed."

"Cristy Root? She wouldn't be related to Garret Root, by any chance?"

"Possibly," he said. "Why? Who's Garret Root?"

"He's the schoolteacher I'm investigating. According to

54

certain rumors, he's an exhibitionist, so the media has instigated a manhunt."

"Odd that I've never heard of the guy."

"So no official complaint against him has been made?"

"Nope. Not a one. But if what you're saying is true, we probably should launch an investigation of our own. A crime as serious as that warrants a closer look."

"I agree, but it does surprise me that the parents of the kid haven't filed a complaint."

"Yeah, you would expect that to be the case," said Chase as he drummed his fingers on his desk. He got up with a swift motion and grabbed his jacket from the back of his chair. "You know what? Why don't you and I go out there right now and look into this thing? And if Garret Root and Cristy Root are related, maybe there's some connection between the two cases. What do you say?"

"I'd say you've got yourself a deal, detective," she said, also getting up. The armchair was so deep and so comfortable that it took her more than one attempt, though, and finally, her husband had to grab her hand and pull her to full perpendicularity. "I have to warn you, though," she said. "My grandmother is also looking into the same thing, so we've got competition."

"I don't consider your grandmother competition," said Chase. "Though your uncle probably won't be happy. He hates it when his mom meddles in police business."

Odelia grinned. "Once upon a time, you hated it when *I* meddled in your investigations, remember?"

"How could I forget?" said Chase with a smile. "And now we're investigating most of our cases together. We've come a long way, babe, wouldn't you say?"

They left the office and almost bumped into Odelia's uncle. "Where are you two off to?" he asked, looking less than pleased. "Don't tell me you're taking an early lunch?"

"We're actually tackling two cases at the same time," said Chase. "Talk about synergy and efficiency, boss."

"Well, that's fine, then," said the Chief, slightly mollified. "And if you can handle a third, I've got a doozy for you. Some joker has been selling cookies to kids that are actually filled with some kind of illegal substance—possibly weed. The parents are frantic—as you can imagine. So if you could spare the time, I want you to go over to the Gordon Jovitt School and smoke him out."

Chase and Odelia shared a look. "That's Garret Root's school," said Odelia.

"What a coincidence," said Chase, arching a meaningful eyebrow. "Or not."

As they walked out of the police station, Chase briefly greeted one of his colleagues, a fresh-faced young man who seemed eager to have a chat with the veteran detective. Chase told him that he'd check in with him later, leaving the young man looking slightly disappointed.

"Who's he?" asked Odelia once they were in the car.

"Oh, just some new kid," said Chase vaguely. "Real eager beaver, I gotta say."

She smiled. "Reminds me of someone I know."

Chase grinned. "Yeah, I guess he does remind me of myself when I was his age. Wants to make detective something bad and is always on my case about partnering up. But like I told him and your uncle: I already got a partner in you, babe."

Even though Odelia wasn't a cop but a civilian consultant, each time they teamed up they got results, and that's what mattered, which is why Uncle Alec allowed their unusual cooperation to continue, in spite of what anyone else said.

Before long, they were en route to the Gordon Jovitt School, located on the other side of town, with Chase behind the wheel of his squad car and Odelia riding shotgun. It felt great to be out on a case again, she thought. Now if only her grandmother wouldn't make a mess of things as she often did...

CHAPTER 12

*J*im's business meeting had gone so well he felt like celebrating. And since he had his brother set up at the house, and his sister mourning the premature end of her engagement, he figured the three siblings might get together that night and have a good old-fashioned family reunion. He might even invite their parents over and turn it into a full-fledged family dinner. He had only launched his new venture eight short months ago, but already customers were lining up to take advantage of his services, paying him handsomely for his particular brand of consultancy. And so the moment he got into his car, he opened the Root family WhatsApp group chat. He still had some business to attend to in connection with the contract he'd just signed, but once that was out of the way, he was ready to party.

The responses from both Garret and Cristy were luke-warm, but that was to be expected after what they had been through that day. But his mom and dad were eager to accept his invitation, and so it looked as if family dinner was a go. He glanced out of his window and saw that his client also got into his car, a shiny brand-new BMW, and drove off. He grinned as he took out his laptop and got busy creating the campaign he and the client had agreed on. And as he focused on working his particular brand of magic, it wasn't long before he got several dings on his phone. When he glanced at the display, he saw that more clients were expressing their eagerness to go into business with him. Ka-ching!

* * *

TRESSA SAT at her desk wondering if she should call Douglas or not. Thoughts of a conflicting nature shot through her mind: she was too old for a man like Douglas. He was too handsome, and she was too much of a plain Jane. Their age difference would make a successful relationship impossible. He probably already had a girlfriend and would make fun of her when she did work up the courage to give him a call. She shouldn't be the one giving him a call. If he really was interested in her, he should be the one calling her. On and on it went, distracting her to the extent that she could hardly get any work done that afternoon.

Bonnie must have noticed how much she was suffering because at some point she leaned over and said, "Just send him a text."

"But what should I say? I have no idea what to say!"

"Just tell him... tell him that you think he's a great barista."

"That sounds too lame," she said with a groan.

"Or tell him that you've been thinking about him all day."

"That's so forward!"

"But it's true, isn't it? You have been thinking about him all day."

"I know, but that doesn't mean I have to tell him. And

besides, he probably wrote down his phone number by mistake."

Bonnie laughed. "How do you figure that?"

"He probably meant to write it on the cup for a different woman, but it ended up on mine, and so if I call him, he'll be embarrassed, and I'll be embarrassed, and then I'll never be able to go near him again!"

"God, you really are overthinking this," said Bonnie with an eye-roll.

They both shut up for a moment as their boss passed by their desks, giving them nasty glances. Bonnie pretended to type something on her computer while Tressa studied the design on her desk very closely indeed. The moment the supervisor had passed, they resumed their conversation. "I know," said Bonnie. "Why don't you pass by the Happy Bean after work? You order another coffee and give Douglas the opportunity to ask you out. Or maybe you can ask him out."

"He'll never ask me out. And I'll be damned if I'm going to ask him out."

"Then maybe I'll do it," Bonnie suggested. "I'll tell him that my friend likes him but is too shy to give him a call."

"Please don't," said Tressa, horrified at the idea.

Bonnie gave her a sweet smile as she placed her chin on her hand. "Look, do you like this guy or not?"

"I do," Tressa admitted. "But—"

"Do you want to get to know him better or not?"

"I do, but he's too young for me and too handsome and—"

But Bonnie waved all her objections away. "Why don't you let him decide?"

She sighed. It sounded like a good idea. But as she thought about stepping up to the guy and suggesting a date, she got a funny feeling in her tummy that she recognized from the last time she'd had to conduct a job interview. Nerves!

"Oh, my god, there he is!" said Bonnie suddenly.

"Ha ha, very funny," said Tressa.

"He's coming this way!"

In spite of her reservations, she still looked up and saw, to her surprise, that her colleague was right: Douglas was heading their way, wending his way through the maze of desks. He was carrying a cup of his superb coffee, and judging from the way he was focused on her, she was the person he was looking for!

In a reflex action, she straightened her hair, checked if she didn't have a smudge on her blouse, and then awaited the inevitable. Finally, the handsome barista reached them and plastered the same wide grin on his face that she knew so well.

"Special delivery for Tressa O'Keefe," he said as he placed the tray on her desk.

"But... I didn't order anything," she said, very lamely, she thought.

"Sometimes we like to reward our best customers with a surprise order," Douglas explained. "And today you're that customer, Tressa—may I call you Tressa?"

"You may," said Tressa, drowning in the man's gaze as he only seemed to have eyes for her. "I've brought you one of our freshly baked bagels as an extra," he explained, "No charge, of course."

She swallowed with difficulty, then said, her voice sounding strange to her own ears, "Douglas, would you like to... I mean, if you have time one of these evenings... would you enjoy having... join me for... go to a resta..."

His grin increased in wattage, if that was even possible, and he said, "Yes to all of the above, Tressa. How about tonight? I know a nice little place just around the corner from the coffee shop that serves the best Italian food."

"That sounds great," she said, much relieved that he was responding with such enthusiasm.

"Shall we say… eight o'clock?"

She nodded.

"Meet you there?"

She nodded again, discovering she had momentarily lost the power of speech.

"Great," he said, getting up from the edge of her desk, where he had momentarily planted his perfectly shaped glutes. "Really looking forward to it, Tressa."

She cleared her throat. "Me, too… Douglas."

He flashed her another smile, and then he was off. But not before expressing a fervent wish that she would enjoy her blend of the Douglas special, as he called it.

"Oh, I will," she said as she watched him leave. In doing so, he was looked after by every single woman in the office, and a lot of the men, too. When he was gone, they all turned to her, and she felt her face glow a very furious red.

"Well done, girl!" said Bonnie, much pleased. "Now drink up, before your Douglas special gets cold!"

"I don't think that's possible," she said, furiously fanning herself.

And then both she and Bonnie burst into a loud bout of giggles.

CHAPTER 13

Clint Bearman shuffled uncomfortably in his chair. His boss had been standing with his back to him for the past five minutes, looking out of the window of his corner office and letting the awkward silence drag on. And since Clint knew better than to break the silence himself, he had no other recourse but to sit there and sweat and feel as uncomfortable as he had ever done in his entire life. As a loyal soldier of Parkland Insurance, he was one of the respectable institution's movers and shakers, and no other salesman could offer such great numbers as he did—earning him the moniker of 'top dog' amongst his colleagues and bosses alike.

But now the top dog seemed to be about to be put out to pasture if the expression on his boss's face when he walked into his office was any indication, or the tone of the email he had received summoning him there.

Finally, the man turned to face him, and it was clear that his face spelled storm.

"When you joined Parkland, you signed your employee handbook."

"Yes, I did, sir," said Clint deferentially.

"One of the stipulations in this handbook referred to the proud history of Parkland Insurance, and also its mission statement, policies, and expectations. We expect all Parkland employees to behave according to certain principles outlined in the handbook, and chief amongst those are adherence to the rule of law and respect for our fellow man. What I'm referring to is a code of conduct."

"Yes, sir," he said, wondering where this was going.

Suddenly his boss pointed at him. "You broke this code of conduct when you joined this group of pet torturers and started sharing the most heinous, egregious and frankly revolting images of pets being hurt in indescribable ways."

He stared at the man. "What?" he said, before he could stop himself.

"Don't play coy with me, Clint!" his boss now thundered, planting both hands on his desk. His face had turned a violent crimson, and spittle flew from his mouth. "You are a disgrace to this company, and I have already instructed our lawyers to determine the extent of the damage your behavior has done to the reputation of the Parkland Group, and make no mistake—we will sue."

"Sue who?" he asked. "What are you talking about?"

The man ground his teeth for a few moments before replying. "Out," he said.

"But sir!"

"Out of my office—out of my company—out of my life! GET! OUT!"

And since he didn't see a lot of options, he got up and hurried out of the office. He still wasn't entirely sure what had happened, but one thing stood out: the fact that he had been summarily dismissed, his employment terminated!

The moment he closed the door of the big chief's office, two burly security men approached him, attached themselves to his arms, and frogmarched him through an office filled with his colleagues, who all gaped at him in abject confusion, and then he was escorted from the building, without getting a chance to even empty his desk or collect his personal belongings.

The moment they arrived in the lobby, they saw to it that his badge was removed from his person, and then they unceremoniously kicked him out of the building and told him never to return!

"But, but, but…" he sputtered as he watched the revolving door through which he had entered his place of work so many times over the course of the past eight years. "But I'm the top dog," he said to no one in particular.

He realized he didn't even have his phone, which he had switched off that morning because he was in a meeting, and which was still lying in a drawer of his desk, no doubt buzzing away with messages from his fiancée. Now how was he going to explain to Cristy that on the eve of their wedding he was suddenly without a job? And if his boss's words were to be believed, he was about to be sued for damages—though he couldn't imagine what damages these could be.

And as he staggered to a nearby bench, some other snippets of this recent conversation drifted into his mind. Pet torturers? Pets being hurt? What the heck?

It didn't take long for one of his colleagues to walk out of the building holding a cardboard box. It contained his phone, his cactus, and the several 'top dog' awards he had amassed over the years. It even contained the framed picture of him and Cristy.

"Thanks, Joe," he said gratefully as he accepted the box.

His colleague took a seat next to him on the bench, and for a moment, they both looked up at the giant glass and concrete tower that had been his home away from home for the past eight years.

"You shouldn't have done it, Clint," said Joe finally.

"Done what?" he asked.

"I mean, I don't like dogs or cats—filthy animals, the whole lot of them. But even I think they should be treated with respect. And some of those pictures…" He made a face. "They just made my stomach turn, you know."

"But… what are you talking about? What dogs? What cats?"

Joe gave him a strange look. "The dogs and cats that you tortured, of course. And then shared the pictures in that Telegram group with your buddies."

"But I never tortured anyone," he said. "There must be some mistake."

"No mistake," said Joe as he took out his own phone. "These are just a couple of the screenshots that your fiancée sent, but they're enough to make me sick."

And then Joe showed him some of the most horrific pictures he'd ever seen. Oddly enough, every one was signed, 'Clint Bearman—master executioner.'

"But that's not me," he said as he scrolled through the images. "I never posted these."

Joe grabbed his phone from his hands and shook his head. "Seriously, bro. If I were you, I'd consider therapy. This stuff is sick—you're sick." And with these words, he got up and hurried back into the building, leaving Clint to stare after him in horror and shock.

He then picked up his phone from the cardboard box perched on his knees and switched it back on. Immediately, a barrage of messages started flashing across the screen— possibly hundreds of them. Several were from his fiancée, but most were from his friends and family. The gist was that he was a sick man, and they wanted nothing more to do with him. As he studied the messages from Cristy, he got the sinking feeling that his marriage was over before it even got started. Even his landlord had sent him a strongly worded message, expecting him to hand in his keys and vacate the property posthaste.

As he flipped through the messages, he realized that his life as he had known it was effectively over. And the worst part was that he had no idea why!

CHAPTER 14

*W*e had finally arrived at the Gordon Jovitt School, and even though strictly speaking we probably weren't allowed inside, Gran being Gran, she didn't think twice about including us as she set foot in the entrance and then headed for the principal's office. Accompanying us were Scarlett, and also a little girl who must have become interested in seeing four cats and two senior citizens stroll through the halls. The little girl's name was Maya, and as she tagged along, she never stopped talking.

"I like cats," she intimated. "I like cats a lot. Not everyone likes cats. My mama doesn't like cats. She says that cats are mean, but I don't agree. And my papa also doesn't agree, and when I asked if I could have a cat, he said no, on account of the fact that mama is allergic to cats, which is probably the reason she calls you mean, since you give her allergies, and one of the meanest things you can do to a person is to give her allergies. So where are you going? Are you going to sign up at the school? Cause I don't think they accept cats as students here at Gordon Jovitt."

It was very difficult to get a word in edgewise, and even

then, I wasn't sure she would understand what we were saying. In that respect, she was quite different from Grace, for instance. But as it turned out, we didn't have to say a thing, for she provided all the conversation.

"I like dogs, too," she told us. "Not as much as cats, but at least dogs don't give mama an allergic reaction. So maybe we'll get a dog when I'm older instead of a cat. Which I guess isn't bad. But I'd still much rather have a cat, of course. So are you available? Can I take one of you home right now? I like big fat cats, so you will do nicely." At this, she placed her grubby little hands on my person, and I had to resist a powerful urge to give her a flick from my paw—claws extended!

But since I'm basically a peaceable cat and don't like to cause trouble, especially in a place where I have the distinct impression I'm not fully welcome, I resisted the urge. Instead, I walked a little faster and even arrived at the principal's office before the rest of our troupe did.

"Okay, so maybe I'll take this small gray one," said the little girl and tried to catch Dooley!

"Hey, lay off," said Gran in a warning tone.

The girl stared at her for a moment, then said, "You're a mean old lady, aren't you?" And with these words, she hurried off, not wanting to be caught by Gran!

"I'm not old," said Gran as she gave the girl's retreating back a glare. But then she forgot about the altercation and proceeded to apply her knuckles to the principal's door and immediately walk in without waiting for a response.

I got the impression that we caught the principal by surprise, for she was looking in a small compact mirror when we entered and applying makeup to her lips. When we entered, she gave us an irate look. "Who are you? You can't just come barging in here."

"My name is Vesta Muffin," said Gran, "and this is Scarlett

Canyon. I'm the leader of the neighborhood watch, and Scarlett is my second-in-command. In that capacity, we're here to conduct an investigation into the behavior of one of your teachers, Garret Root. Rumor has it that Mr. Root has behaved inappropriately toward his pupils, and as the neighborhood watch, it is our responsibility to follow up on any nefarious activities conducted."

The woman stared at Gran with a look of surprise on her face. "Who told you about that?"

Gran raised her chin defiantly. "As your neighborhood watch, it is our job to know everything. So what can you tell us about the alleged incident?"

The woman thought for a moment, then said, "There's nothing alleged about it. Mr. Root exposed himself to one of his students. The girl told her mother, and we took measures to make sure it wouldn't happen again. As for the rest of the story, that's for the police to decide, not the school. And most certainly not the neighborhood watch," she added for good measure.

"What if I told you that Garret Root vehemently denies the allegations?"

The principal frowned, cutting a deep groove between her suspiciously dark brows. "Have you spoken to Garret?"

"We have."

"Look, this whole business is out of my hands now. If Garret feels he's been unjustly treated, he should seek legal advice and consult with a lawyer."

"According to what Garret told us, he was off on vacation when this all came to pass," Gran continued. "He hasn't even been officially made aware of any allegations leveled against his person."

"I gave him a call and the school has sent him a letter," said the principal with a wave of the hand. "Now if you would please leave my office."

"So who's the person who made the complaint?"

"I really have nothing further to say to you. Now please leave."

"According to Garret, a fellow teacher named Melody Jarram made up this whole story to get back at him for spurning her advances."

The principal gave Gran a look of incredulity. "Will you please leave? Now!"

"Oh, fine," said Gran. "But don't say I didn't warn you."

"Warn me of what?!" asked the woman with a gesture of exasperation. It's one of the chief hallmarks of Gran's style of communication that she often leaves her audience reeling and reaching for their preferred stimulants in the form of a stiff drink.

"Malfeasance, for one thing. And wrongful dismissal for another."

"Garret hasn't been dismissed. Yet. He's been temporarily suspended until we can get to the bottom of this whole business with the inappropriate behavior. And if he really wants to address the issue, he should do so in person and not send the neighborhood watch to do his bidding. And now please leave before I'm obliged to have you forcibly removed from my office."

"Very well," said Gran. "But I will have you know that I'm doing so under protest." She wagged a finger in the woman's direction. "This isn't over, missy. Not by a long shot!"

With these words, we finally made our leave, before we were kicked out. At least we had learned one thing: Garret hadn't been fired yet. He had been temporarily suspended pending further inquiries into the allegations leveled against his person.

Gran wasn't happy with the way her recent interview with the principal had gone, for as we traversed the hallways of the school, she said, "Something very fishy is going on here, Scarlett. Something very fishy indeed!"

"The exit is that way, Vesta," said Scarlett, pointing in the other direction.

"But we're not going there, are we?" said Gran, giving her a clever look.

"Where are we going?"

"To find Melody Jarram, of course. The person who framed Garret!"

CHAPTER 15

$\mathcal{O}$delia and Chase swung into the office of Garret Root's school's principal to find the woman looking extremely perturbed. "This is the second time today that someone barges in here asking questions about Mr. Root," she said, eyeing them sternly across half-moon-shaped glasses and giving Odelia a sudden flashback to her own school days and the times she had been called into the principal's office because she had been up to something morally reprehensible like chewing gum in class or dying her hair a vivid pink.

"Who was the other person?" asked Chase.

"Um... some ladies from the neighborhood watch," said the principal, whose name was Hillary Hollins. "And they were very insistent, too. In fact, I had to threaten to have them forcibly removed from my office before they finally agreed to leave. Most disturbing, I have to say."

Odelia shared a look with her husband. Looked like Gran and Scarlett had beaten them to it. But since theirs was official police business, they didn't allow the principal to browbeat them and instead drew out a pair of chairs and took a seat.

"So about this Garret Root business," said Chase. "The odd thing is that we haven't received any official complaint. But since the papers are full of the story and Garret Root's face is plastered all across the front pages of even our national newspapers, my boss thought it important to launch an official inquiry anyway."

"So what can you tell us about the allegations?" asked Odelia, taking out her digital notepad and her stylus.

"Not much, I'm afraid," said the principal. "We received an anonymous complaint from one of the parents that Garret Root exposed himself to one of his female pupils. So naturally we immediately took measures to ensure that this wouldn't happen again and suspended Garret until further notice."

"An anonymous complaint, you say," said Chase. "So you have no idea who this pupil was? Or who the parent is who made the complaint?"

"Not at this moment," the principal admitted. "But we have notified the school psychologist, and we will conduct the necessary interviews with all of Mr. Root's pupils and try to get to the bottom of this very troubling incident. Furthermore, we want to make sure that there are no other incidents that haven't been reported yet, and to that end we have notified all the parents of all the students and asked them to talk to their children and try to ascertain whether this was an isolated incident or whether it's part of a pattern of behavior."

"So why haven't you made a formal complaint with the police department?" asked Chase.

The principal waved an ineffectual hand. "We thought it better to postpone until we had possession of actual facts as opposed to this one anonymous complaint. Since we haven't been able to identify the victim yet, we thought it prudent to wait."

"In other words: you were more concerned with the reputation of your school than the damage this could do to your students," said Chase.

Principal Hollins bridled at these words. "Absolutely not! Of course we will make a formal complaint against Garret Root, but first we need to know exactly what is going on. Surely you can appreciate our desire for thoroughness."

Chase nodded. "So you have suspended Garret Root until further notice?"

"Yes, we have. Pending further inquiries, we have suspended him and asked him not to come anywhere near his students. In the meantime, we are conducting a full-scale investigation, the outcome of which will determine further actions."

"Don't you find it odd that these parents would lodge a complaint with the school but not go to the police?" asked Odelia.

The principal shrugged. "We are the first point of contact, and also, they trust us. Some of these people have had a bad experience with the police, and they'd much rather work with us than with you. So no, I don't find that odd at all. And once we have identified the victim, we will, of course, advise them to come forward and file an official complaint against the teacher."

"Okay, something else entirely," said Chase, tapping his notebook with his pencil. "According to a person who has come forward, a group of kids selling cookies for a school fundraiser were caught selling spiked cookies. According to lab analyses, the cookies contained weed. So what can you tell us about that?"

The principal stared at Chase as if seeing a ghost. "Spiked

cookies? Weed? I'm sure there must be some kind of mistake."

"No mistake," said Chase curtly. "The cookies were confiscated and were shown to contain an illegal substance. So now we're trying to ascertain who supplied the cookies and whether they were accidentally spiked or on purpose."

"And someone ate those cookies?" asked the principal.

"That's right, but as soon as they did, they decided that they tasted funny, so they immediately wrapped them up and brought them to the police station."

The principal frowned. "I find that very odd indeed—to use your term. Now why would anyone file a complaint against a group of kids selling cookies?"

"The point you're missing," said Chase, sitting up a little straighter, "is that the cookies were proven to contain an illegal substance. Unfortunately, the person who bought the cookies couldn't identify the kids in question, only that they were five little girls from the Gordon Jovitt School, so could you please advise as to who these kids could be and why they're selling marijuana-laced cookies?"

The principal sat mum for a moment, clearly aghast at these allegations. "I can assure you that our pupils are not in the business of peddling drugs," she said stiffly. "Be that as it may, of course I will advise you as to the identity of these girls. Melody Jarram is the person in charge of this year's fundraiser activities, and it's mainly her class that has taken the lead in the selling of the cookies."

"Where can we find this Melody Jarram?" asked Chase, getting up.

"I'll walk you over to her class," said the principal. "But I can assure you that Mrs. Jarram is a perfectly respectable teacher who would never be involved in anything as heinous as lacing cookies with drugs and then asking her students to sell them to the general public."

"Who bakes the cookies?" asked Odelia as they followed the principal out of her office and down the corridor.

"Um… you would have to ask Melody. Last year we had a parent whose husband is a professional baker provide the batches. This year… I think Melody said something about a friend of hers who was going to do the baking." She shook her head. "This is all very distressing. Very distressing indeed. Well, here we are."

They had arrived at a classroom, and the principal waved at the teacher through the window. Mrs. Jarram, a middle-aged teacher with oversized glasses, an overbite, and an abundance of copper-colored curly hair, immediately stopped explaining the ill-fated Russian campaign of Napoleon Bonaparte and came to the door. Walking out into the corridor, she gave Odelia and Chase a curious look.

"These people are with the police department," Principal Hollins explained. "There seems to be a problem with the cookies for this year's fundraiser?"

Mrs. Jarram turned a pair of very large eyes to them. "A problem with the cookies? Oh, dear. I knew they were over-baked. I even told Natalie, but she insisted that's what the recipe said. I tasted them myself and thought they were too hard. Did someone go and chip a tooth?"

"Do you have a last name for this Natalie?" asked Chase.

"Natalie Francis. She's our main provider for the cookies this year. She came highly recommended by last year's baker, who owns a bakery but was slammed with work and couldn't squeeze in an extra batch this year. So what happened?"

As Chase explained the spiked cookie allegations, they saw Melody's eyes go even wider. "Spiked!" she cried as she brought a distraught hand to her face. "But that's impossible! I tasted them myself and they were fine!"

"You experienced no adverse effects from the cookies?" asked Odelia.

NIC SAINT

"None at all. Oh dear, oh dear, oh dear." She turned to the principal, who stood listening with tightly pressed lips. "This is a disaster!" she said, close to tears now.

"Have all the cookies been sold?" asked Chase.

"All of them! They were extremely successful. Some people bought several bags. Said they were so delicious they couldn't stop eating them."

It certainly was one way to guarantee a successful campaign, Odelia thought. Spike your cookies and get people hooked. Though judging from the way Melody Jarram was falling apart right before their eyes, it was clear that she had no idea.

"Okay, so to get to the bottom of this, we need to talk to Natalie Francis," said Chase. "Do you have her contact details?"

And as Mrs. Jarram took out her phone and provided them with the parent's phone number and address, she looked on the verge of a mental breakdown, causing Odelia to assure her that no one was blaming her for anything. After all, she couldn't reasonably have known that someone had spiked the cookies.

"But I tasted them!" said Mrs. Jarram. "And they were fine!"

"We believe you," said Odelia. "And we will get to the bottom of this."

"There's also the matter of Garret Root," said Chase, causing Mrs. Jarram to look even more distressed than she already was. "What can you tell us about him?"

"Not much," said the teacher. "Only the rumors I've heard about inappropriate behavior toward his students. He has been suspended, hasn't he?"

The principal nodded. "Suspended while we look into this most distressing incident."

"The fact of the matter is that Garret Root has issued

78

certain allegations aimed against you, Mrs. Jarram," said Odelia.

The woman's jaw dropped. "Against me!"

"He claims that you are behind these rumors."

"What?!!!"

"According to Mr. Root, you have harbored certain romantic notions toward him," Chase continued, picking up the baton, "and he has been forced to spurn those notions on more than one occasion, causing you to adopt a powerful resentment against him and instigate these rumors that have no basis in fact."

"As a way of taking revenge on him," Odelia supplied, giving the woman a look of concern and hoping she wouldn't collapse on them any moment now.

The teacher's face had gone very pale, but suddenly flushed an angry red. Her eyes blazed, and as she adjusted her glasses, she launched into a powerful rebuke of Garret's accusations. "I have *no* idea where you get your information, officer," she said, her voice taking on a measured tone. "But I can assure you it's *all* lies. I have *never* been in love with Garret Root, and I certainly have *never* been spurned by him. So the whole idea that I would start a rumor against him is simply *preposterous*."

"Garret claims that he's innocent and that someone is organizing a smear campaign against him."

"Me?!" Mrs. Jarram cried. "*I'm* organizing a smear campaign against Garret?! The man has gone *mad*! We're *colleagues*. Nothing more. If anything, *he's* the one who's been harboring certain feelings for me that are deeper than mere friendship. *He's* the one who tried to kiss *me*! I've ignored it, but if this is how he wants to play it, I will file a complaint against *him* for harassment in the workplace!" She turned to the principal. "Hillary, I don't have to stand for this, do I? I mean, do I?"

"No, you don't, Melody," the principal assured her. "You most certainly do not."

The teacher raised her head defiantly. "Well, then." She eyed Odelia closely. "Officer…"

"Actually, I'm not with the police," Odelia specified.

"Odelia is a civilian consultant," Chase added.

The teacher wasn't deterred. "Officer Odelia, I wish to file an official complaint against Garret Root for sexual harassment in the workplace." Her chin tilted even higher as twin circles of a bright crimson appeared on her cheeks. "At last year's Christmas party, he tried to kiss me. On the lips, if you please! On my lips!"

"Oh, dear," the principal murmured as she shook her head in shock.

CHAPTER 16

The maze of corridors in the Gordon Jovitt School was impressive, to such an extent that by the time we had finally found where Melody Jarram was hiding, Odelia and Chase had beaten us to it. The moment we rounded the corner, we saw them interviewing Mrs. Jarram, in the presence of the principal.

The four of us wanted to join them, but Gran held us back.

"Stay put!" she warned us in no uncertain terms.

"But Gran, don't you want to hear what they have to say?"

"We can listen perfectly fine from here," she said. And so we retreated to the safety of the corridor and listened carefully. So by the time Mrs. Jarram revealed the identity of the cookie spiker, Gran wrote it all down.

"I didn't even know that cookies were being spiked," Scarlett whispered.

"Odelia has been holding out on us," said Gran. "But two can play that game!"

"Oh, boy," said Brutus. "Looks like we're in competition with Odelia now."

"Yeah, looks like it," I agreed.

We listened for more juicy tidbits of information, but apart from the fact that Mrs. Jarram decided to file a complaint against Garret for kissing her on the lips during a Christmas party, not much else was revealed.

We watched as Odelia and Chase took their leave, and for a moment, Gran and Scarlett convened to decide on their next course of action. "I'll bet that cookie spike business is connected with the Garret Root case," Gran said.

"In what way?" asked Scarlett.

"The same person who's been exposing himself to those kids must be the one who's been spiking those cookies." She gave Scarlett a meaningful look. "Clearly, there's a rogue teacher on the loose. A perverted drug addict!"

"Do you think it's Garret Root?" asked Scarlett, looking horrified.

"I'm not sure," said Gran pensively. "He didn't strike me as a drug addict. But then I guess you never know." She tapped her notebook. "We need to talk to this Natalie Francis woman. If what that teacher said is true, she's the one who spiked those cookies. Or at the very least knows who did. Let's go!"

And so we went on our way, making sure we didn't bump into Odelia and Chase, who apparently had turned into the competition now.

Before long, and after a lot of going down wrong passage-ways and ending up in dead ends, we found the exit and were right back where we started: inside Gran's little car, going over the facts as they pertained to the case.

To be honest, we hadn't learned a great deal. Except that the Gordon Jovitt School clearly had some issues to contend with.

"Don't you think we should talk to Melody Jarram?" asked Scarlett.

"No need," said Gran. "Odelia and Chase talked to her, and from what I could tell, that woman is a tough cookie. If she's the spider in this web of deceit and malfeasance, she will never talk. No, we need to handle this in a more circuitous way. First let's get some dirt on the woman, and then we can crack her like a nut."

We all gulped a little. Cracking people like nuts wasn't exactly part of our job description. But then again, maybe Gran was right. If Garret Root was innocent, it stood to reason that someone had it in for him, and so far the only lead we had was Melody Jarram—and this mysterious baking parent named Natalie Francis.

And so before long, we were en route to the baking maven, who might or might not have a lucrative sideline as a dealer of weed-spiked cookies.

"Don't you think we should all work together, Gran?" Harriet suggested. "You and Scarlett and Odelia and Chase?"

"It's Odelia who threw down the gauntlet, not me," said Gran, though, to be honest, I had no idea what gauntlet she could possibly be referring to. "The main thing is to get there first, and since Chase got the bigger car and the flashy light, we need to cut some corners, gang." And as we held on for dear life, she pushed down on the accelerator until she was racing along the streets, and as we looked on in horror, she suddenly turned onto the street where the park is located, but instead of going around it, she plowed straight through!

"But Gran!" said Brutus. "You can't drive here!"

But the old lady was too busy racing across the serpentine sandy pathways to bother listening to our friend's sound advice.

"Vesta, are you sure?" asked Scarlett.

"Shut up and watch out for those annoying park rangers," Gran hissed.

The park rangers weren't the problem. The people

walking their dogs who were forced to jump out of the way of Gran's oncoming car were. As they did, they pounded the roof of the car in anger, but in spite of all of that, we probably would have made it, if not suddenly a woman pushing a stroller entered our flight path. For a moment, she simply stood there, clearly not believing what she was seeing when this crazy old lady in a little red car came zooming right at her!

"Get out of the way!" Gran screamed.

But too late. Luckily, Gran's reflexes were a lot better than I would have given her credit for, so instead of hitting the woman with the stroller head-on, she diverted from the path at the last minute, rocketed down a steep incline, and moments later, we were plunged headlong into the pond.

When we left the car through the open window and swam to shore, a duck gave me a not-so-friendly look. "This pond is for ducks only," the duck announced haughtily. "And strictly prohibited for cats!"

"Tell that to Gran," said Harriet as we all valiantly made our way to shore.

Five minutes later, the six of us were standing on the edge of the picturesque duck pond and watching how the little red Peugeot slowly sank to the bottom.

"I don't think we'll beat Odelia and Chase," said Scarlett sadly as she plucked her shirt from her chest and removed a piece of pond scum from her hair.

"We could have made it," said Gran, "if that woman hadn't decided to stop us." She shook an irate fist at the lady, who stood talking to a park ranger. "Saboteur!"

Moments later, the park ranger made his way over to where we were standing, his notebook in his hand. I had a feeling a very hefty fine was about to be issued.

CHAPTER 17

*A*fter our unfortunate swim in the pond, it was obvious that our mission had hit a snag. And so while Gran and Scarlett tussled with the park ranger, we decided to lick our proverbial wounds and find a place to recover from the harrowing adventure.

"Gran really isn't great at this sleuthing business, is she, Max?" asked Dooley.

"No, I think it's safe to say she is pretty bad at it," I agreed.

The four of us had found a place to allow our precious coats to dry in the sun, and as we lay there and watched the world go by, we saw that a sizable collection of lookie-loos had gathered by the pond, eager to save every last aspect of the disaster for posterity by holding up their phones and filming the whole thing.

"So let's recap," said Harriet as she eyed her precious fur with a sense of sadness. Cats in general are fussy about their personal appearance, but Persians even more so, and she didn't like her new look. "We've got a teacher who's being accused of exposing himself to his students, a parent who's accused of spiking her cookies with weed, and a teacher who's accusing Garret of kissing her at a Christmas party and filing a complaint. Am I missing anything?"

"That seems to sum it up nicely," I said.

"So where does all of that leave us?" asked Brutus as he flicked a piece of moss from his person. "I mean, Odelia hasn't asked us to participate in her investigation, and Gran's investigation is obviously a bust, so I'm guessing we're not involved in this in any official capacity anymore?"

"No, I guess not," I said.

He gave us a sunny smile. "So we're off the hook, you guys! No investigation means we can all go home and relax."

"If that means we won't be dunked in a filthy pond, I'm all for it," said Harriet.

"I thought I was going to drown," Dooley intimated. "I don't like being dunked in a dirty pond, Max. It was not a fun experience."

"I'm sure it won't happen again," I told my friend.

"And I'm sure it will," said Brutus. "Unless we officially recuse ourselves from this case."

"But we can't officially recuse ourselves," said Dooley. "Gran asked us to assist her, and she hasn't dropped the investigation yet."

"Oh, she will," said Harriet as she threw a dirty look in Gran's direction. The old lady stood shouting at the park ranger now, obviously not agreeing with the man's assertions. And as we watched, he handed her what looked like a ticket.

It wasn't long before she came stomping in our direction, followed by her friend Scarlett. "Can you believe this!" she said. "This man has the gall—the absolute gall!—to fine the leader of the neighborhood watch! I told him we were conducting official watch business, but do you think he cares? Do you think he bothers? No, of course not! Officious pencil pusher."

She glanced back at the park ranger, who was on the phone now, no doubt eager to get this car removed from his pond and evicted from his nice park.

"Looks like our investigation is a bust," said Scarlett sadly. She then crouched down next to us and said, "I'm sorry, you guys. It's not a lot of fun getting wet, is it?" She gestured at herself. "Trust me, I know exactly how you feel."

"She does look like a drowned chicken," said Harriet with a slight giggle. "And so does Gran. Two drowned chickens and four drowned rats."

I guess the latter referred to the four of us, and she had a point. I don't know if you've ever seen a wet cat, but it's not a sight for sore eyes, let me tell you.

"We should probably get back to the house," said Gran now. "Take a shower and find a fresh set of clothes. And we're going to need some new wheels."

Scarlett gave her a look of incredulity. "You're not seriously suggesting we continue our investigation, are you?"

"Of course we're continuing our investigation!" said Gran. "A man is depending on us, Scarlett. And I, for one, am not the kind of person to back down when faced with a minor hurdle."

"We lost the car!" said Scarlett. "And we almost drowned!"

"Oh, just a swim in the pond," said Gran. "Very refreshing on a warm day. So let's go home, get showered and dressed, and get out there to get to the bottom of this most intriguing case."

But Scarlett shook her head. "No way," she said. And when Gran eyed her with astonishment, she added, "I mean, I'm all for the neighborhood watch and doing the right thing, but let's face it. Your crazy antics have just lost us this case!"

"But Scarlett!" said Gran.

But her friend had started to walk away. "I'm sorry, Vesta. But I draw the line at being thrown into a dirty pond! My hair, my clothes—I have tadpoles in my cleavage! It tickles!" And with these words, she was off, much to Gran's surprise.

"But..." she said weakly. "But but but..." Then she glanced down at the four of us and said, "At least you're still with me, aren't you?"

But Harriet shook her head. "I'm sorry, Gran, but personally I draw the line at almost drowning. So I'm afraid you're on your own from now on."

And she followed Scarlett's example by removing herself from the scene, quickly followed by Brutus, who yelled, "Wait for me, sugar cakes!"

And so finally it was just me, Dooley, and Gran.

"Okay, fine," I told our human. "We'll stick with you. But please promise us to drive more carefully next time, all right? It's not a lot of fun to get wet like this."

"I promise," said Gran, who frankly looked a little crestfallen, I thought.

"So what do you want to do, Gran?" asked Dooley.

"I don't know," Gran confessed as she took a seat next to us.

For a moment, the three of us just sat there, but then all of a sudden, Wilbur Vickery walked past, looking extremely agitated for some reason.

"Wilbur!" Gran yelled. "Over here!"

Wilbur glanced around for a moment, and when he spotted us, he came stalking over. "I've been canceled!" he cried, quite without preamble.

"Canceled? What are you talking about?" asked Gran.

"Some woman has started this rumor that I attacked her, and now there's a mob in front of my store, and they're not allowing anyone to enter!"

"What woman?" asked Gran. "What mob?"

"I don't know what woman," said Wilbur as he took a seat next to us. "It's all over the internet, apparently. She claims that I groped her in the produce section. Can you believe it? Me! Groping a woman in my own store!"

"Are you sure that didn't happen?" asked Gran. "I mean, we all know what you're like, Wilbur. You do like the ladies a little too much, don't you? And to be honest, they don't like you."

Once upon a time, Gran had dated Wilbur. Suffice it to say it had not gone well.

He sagged a little. "Okay, so I do like women, but I would never grope anyone." He dragged a hand through his hair. "And the worst part is that it's all anonymous. There's nothing official. No complaint. Just a lot of rumors."

She clapped him on the back. "At least now you can join us on our investigation. We're looking into allegations made against a schoolteacher." She frowned. "In fact, his case sounds a lot like yours. A lot of rumors but no official complaint being made. And he's been canceled—just like you."

"I don't like being canceled," said Wilbur.

"What's being canceled?" asked Dooley.

"I'm not sure," I said. "But it sounds as if certain rumors cause a person to lose his job or his business." Though of course in both cases those rumors could prove to be correct.

And as Wilbur continued to pour his lament into Gran's listening ears, a familiar figure came shuffling past. It was Kingman, and like his master, he did not look very happy.

"Kingman!" I said, trying to attract his attention.

When Kingman saw us, his face lit up and he came hurrying over. When he approached us, he sniffed and grimaced. "You guys smell funny."

"We were in the duck pond," Dooley explained.

"Not by choice," I hastened to add.

Kingman sagged down next to us. "Something terrible happened," he said.

89

"Yeah, we heard," I said. "Wilbur just told us how he's been canceled."

"Oh, that's what that was all about. I was wondering why all the shouting and screaming. Well, I can certainly relate because I've been canceled too."

We both stared at our friend. "Wait, you've been canceled?" I asked.

"Looks like," said Kingman. "I've been suspended from cat choir and been told not to go anywhere near certain cats—though I have no idea who they are."

"But why?" I asked.

He shrugged. "Beats me. Apparently, there's a rumor circulating that I've made lewd comments to certain female members of our local cat community. Though try as I might, I can't recall ever making such comments to anyone."

"What comments?" asked Dooley, interested. "What lute?"

Kingman gave me a quick look, then said, "Um... I'm not sure, Dooley. The person relaying the information didn't give me any details. They did tell me that there's a general rule being instigated to cast me out of the community. Cats are being advised not to go near me or talk to me or be seen with me. And like I said, Shanille has already told me in no uncertain terms that I'm out of cat choir."

"But that's terrible," I said. "And all because of some rumors?"

He nodded sadly. "They are some very persistent rumors, Max." He gave me a smile. "At least you guys are still talking to me. So you haven't heard anything?"

"No, we haven't," I said. "And if you like, we could investigate and find out who started these rumors? And find out what's at the bottom of them?"

"You probably shouldn't bother. Shanille told me that from now on I'm kryptonite. No cat will come near me for fear of being infected and cast out as well. So my advice to you: let's not be seen together, unless you want to suffer the same fate."

I placed a paw on his shoulder. "We'll get to the bottom of this, Kingman. I promise."

"I didn't know you played the lute, Kingman," said Dooley.

Kingman grimaced and promptly burst into tears.

Dooley gave me a look of astonishment. "Was it something I said?"

"It's just that you're being so kind to me," said the voluminous cat.

And so suddenly we were faced with not one but two friends who had been canceled. Coming on top of the schoolteacher being accused of some very bad behavior, it was starting to look as if the virus was spreading—and spreading fast!

CHAPTER 18

Odelia and Chase had just parked across the street from Natalie Francis's house, fully intent on aiming a few tough questions at the wannabe baker when the cop's phone chimed, and he saw that Odelia's uncle wanted to have a word with him. "Yeah, Chief," he said as he picked up.

Odelia had been checking her notes and preparing for the interview when she noticed that her husband had suddenly gone very still. She looked up and saw that his face revealed that he was in the grip of a very powerful emotion.

"What?" he suddenly exclaimed. "But boss!"

She frowned and gave him a curious look.

"But I swear to God I didn't—"

What was going on?

Finally, he seemed to grind his teeth for a moment before saying, "I understand. Yes, I will hand in my badge and gun. But can't I first interview this... Okay, fine. No, I get it." And as he hung up, she saw that he had a sort of dazed look on his face. He then turned to her. "I've just been suspended, babe."

"What?" she said. "But why?"

He shook his head slowly, like a punch-drunk boxer. "I'm

not sure. Something about an anonymous complaint being made against me. Pending further inquiries, the Chief says he has no other choice but to bench me for the time being. I'm to hand in my gun and badge and go home."

"But what about the investigation?"

"Someone else is taking over."

"But who filed this complaint against you? And what is the complaint?"

"I wish I knew," he said, suddenly slumping in his seat. He rubbed the side of his face. "I've been there before, and I can tell it's serious."

Once upon a time, a complaint had been made against Chase, back when he was still with the NYPD. Later on, the complaint had been proven false, but it had wreaked havoc on the state of mind of the proud detective and had wrecked his career—at least until he had moved to Hampton Cove and Uncle Alec had decided to give him a second chance.

He started up the car. "We better get back," he said.

"But what about Natalie Francis?"

"She can wait. The other guy will handle it from now on." He gave her a sad look. "If you want to continue the investigation, it's on your own dime. With me being benched, your uncle told me he's rescinding any privileges you've been granted for the time being. So no more civilian consultants. You're just a civilian from now on."

"I don't believe this," said Odelia. "Can he just do that?"

"He just did," said the cop curtly, and drove off.

She thought for a moment to go against her uncle's wishes, but saw that it wouldn't do her husband's career a lot of good if she did. It was best to await the results of the investigation. She was sure that whatever it was, it would be thrown out as soon as it was subjected to a closer scrutiny. Chase was nothing if not a diligent cop, and whoever had made this complaint against him would be proven wrong.

"I don't understand how you can be punished before proven guilty," she said. "It just seems wrong."

"I guess that's the way it goes," he said. "Your uncle doesn't want to be seen playing favorites just because I married his niece. Perception is everything, babe."

"I know, but you've never set a foot wrong, and your arrest record is exemplary. So can't he give you the benefit of the doubt for now?"

He grimaced. "Guess not."

Before long, they were back where they had started, and Chase parked in front of the police station. He sat there staring at his car keys for a moment. "I better hand these in as well. Which means we won't have a ride for the time being."

"I still have my dinged-up old pickup," she reminded him. "And we've got my mom's old Peugeot."

But as they sat there, a flatbed truck passed by, and as she glanced over, she thought she saw that same old Peugeot hauled up onto the bed of the truck. She blinked, but when she opened her eyes again, the car was still there. And if she wasn't mistaken, it looked as if it had suffered some water damage for some reason. Which couldn't be right, of course.

"Wish me luck," said Chase as he opened the door.

"Oh, I'm coming with you," she said. "I want to have a word with my uncle about this nonsense."

"Better not," he advised. "We don't want to make matters worse."

She didn't see how much worse they could get but did as he asked and decided to stay out of it. For now.

And as she took a seat on a bench to wait for her husband to return, she saw how that same young cop who had addressed them earlier came walking out of the station, looked around until he had located the squad car they had just vacated, smiled as he walked over, and opened the car with the same keys Chase must have just handed in.

It looked like this kid was the detective taking over the spiked cookies case. Well, good for him, she thought. And as she fought the urge to give her uncle a piece of her mind, she saw a strange procession approach: it was her grandmother, accompanied by Wilbur Vickery and Max, Dooley, and Kingman. For some reason, Gran looked as if she had just taken a dip in a pond, and so did Max and Dooley.

She waved, and the group came over.

"What happened to you?" she asked her grandmother.

"Don't ask," said Gran. She gestured to the police station. "Dolores in?"

"I guess so," said Odelia. "Why?"

"Wilbur here has been canceled," said Gran, much to Odelia's surprise. "So we want to file a complaint against the complainers. You know, give them a taste of their own medicine. See if we can't get the cancelers canceled."

She eyed the shopkeeper more closely and saw how morose and dejected he looked. "I've been canceled," he confirmed morosely. "And I've been forced to close down my shop. So if you've got any advice for me, I sure could use some."

"Kingman has also been canceled," Max announced.

"And he's taken up playing the lute," Dooley added.

She frowned. "There seems to be a lot of that going around. Chase just got suspended because someone filed an anonymous complaint against him."

"Chase is being canceled?" asked Gran. "But why?"

"No idea. My uncle wouldn't say."

Gran's face took on a mutinous expression as she balled her fists. "Oh, we'll see about that!" she said, and before Odelia could stop her, she was setting foot for the police station. And since she didn't want to sit there twiddling her thumbs, she decided to follow suit. Frankly speaking, she wanted answers, and if her uncle didn't want to give them, she'd go out there and find them herself.

"It's a nice instrument, the lute," Dooley commented as he, Max, and Kingman followed behind their humans. "It's a little bit like a guitar, isn't it, only smaller?"

"Oh, Dooley," said Kingman with a sigh.

CHAPTER 19

$\mathcal{I}$t was an unusual procession that marched through the police station vestibule and past Dolores, the desk sergeant. She eyed us strangely, but since she was on the phone, couldn't give us the benefit of her usual sharp-tongued wit. Instead, she merely frowned as we passed by her desk.

Inside the police station proper, the usual noise and business assaulted our sensitive ears, and as we went in search of Odelia's uncle, we passed by Chase's office and saw that the stalwart cop was cleaning out his desk, relegating his meager belongings and personal items to a cardboard box.

"Oh, no, you don't!" said Gran as she watched the scene.

"Did you hand in your badge and gun?" asked Odelia.

Chase nodded. He looked like a kicked puppy, so I could only imagine the tongue-lashing his superior officer must have doled out. But when we entered the Chief's office, we found the big man looking just as downcast as his deputy.

"What do you want?" he growled when we filed into his office.

"I want you to reinstate Chase," said Gran, not beating about the bush as is her habit.

"I can't," he said. "Certain allegations have been made against him that leave me no other choice than to suspend him." He sighed deeply. "And the worst part is that now I have to assign someone to investigate him. My own godson!"

"What's the complaint?" asked Odelia.

He gave her a guarded look. "I can't tell you—it's confidential."

"You know as well as I do that this is just a bunch of nonsense, Alec," said Gran. "These allegations are obviously a load of baloney. So why don't you simply dismiss them out of hand?" She had placed her hands flat on her son's desk and was pinning the chief of police down with a look that brooked no contest.

"I can't," said Uncle Alec. "Every complaint made against an officer of the law must be taken seriously. An inquiry has to be launched, and as long as the investigation is pending, the officer has to be suspended. Those are the rules."

"Oh, this is just too much," said Gran as she plunked herself down on a chair. "First Wilbur being canceled and now Chase. What is the world coming to?"

Uncle Alec gave Wilbur a look of commiseration. "You've been canceled, too?"

"I have," the shopkeeper confirmed. "Someone lodged a complaint against me, and there's some kind of online campaign to boycott the store."

Odelia had taken out her phone and nodded. "It's true. There's even a petition campaign to permanently close down the store. It says Wilbur is a known sex pest, and as long as he's allowed to continue monetizing his sex pestery and make a living by operating his store, no woman in this town will ever feel safe again."

"Has anyone filed an official complaint against Wilbur?" asked Gran.

"Not that I know of," said the Chief as he patted his head, where only a few straggling hairs remained and held on for dear life. "Why, what did you do?"

"Nothing!" said Wilbur. "This whole thing just came out of the blue. And the worst part is that I have no idea who's behind the complaint—if there even is a complaint. All I know is that I've been receiving threats and that my store was vandalized."

"Vandalized?" asked Odelia.

Wilbur nodded sadly. "Someone spray-painted some very nasty things about me all across the window, and they also left a pile of garbage. They also dumped a dummy and set it on fire. I suppose that dummy represents me, though I have to say it doesn't look like me at all. More like Ken from Barbie."

"You should file a complaint against those vandals," said Odelia. "And also against the people who've launched this petition and this online hate campaign."

"What good would that do?" said Wilbur. "It's all online, and you know as well as I do that it's very difficult to capture these people—they're like ghosts."

Uncle Alec had been nodding absentmindedly until Gran turned to him. "Don't just sit there, Alec. Do something!"

"What do you want me to do?!" said the Chief, spreading his arms.

"I don't know—something! You," she said, pointing at Wilbur. "You file an official complaint against these bullies. And you," she said, pointing at her son, "go after whoever is harassing the good people of this town for no good reason at all."

Wilbur nodded, but he didn't seem entirely convinced that it would do him a lot of good. "Okay, fine," he said. "I will file a complaint. But that still won't stop this campaign. And as long as that petition isn't taken down, I'm afraid to leave the house—or to open my store."

"Who's going to look into this complaint that's been made against Chase?" asked Odelia.

"I've given it to Wade Westen," said Uncle Alec. "He's a good kid, and he's assured me that he will get to the bottom of this thing."

"Did you also give him the spiked cookies case?"

"I did, yeah. And this business of the schoolteacher displaying inappropriate behavior, um..." He snapped his fingers in an effort to jog his memory.

"Garret Root," Odelia supplied helpfully.

"That's the one. So what I would advise is for all of you to go home and await further developments. As you can tell, I've got the case well in hand, and I'm sure that once Wade gets to the bottom of what's going on, exactly, we'll discover it's all been one big misunderstanding."

Oddly enough, even though he tried to project a modicum of confidence, I had the distinct impression that the Chief didn't believe his own words.

Which told me we were in big trouble.

CHAPTER 20

*T*ex had seen his last patient of the day and breathed a sigh of relief. Even after all these years, he still enjoyed his chosen profession, but sometimes he wished that his patients would use common sense in determining their symptoms instead of rushing to pay him a visit at the least little sign of trouble. Take Ida Baumgartner, for instance, who seemed to have cornered the market on imaginary diseases. Today she had insisted that she was suffering from a rare type of kidney cancer that manifested as a horseshoe-shaped rash on the forehead. It was true that she had a small rash on her brow, and with some imagination—or actually a lot—one could perhaps interpret its shape as vaguely resembling a tiny horseshoe. But to go from that to deciding she only had three more months to live was far-fetched, to say the least. But when he had tried to tell her she had no cause for concern, she had accused him of being a lousy doctor and threatened to take him to court.

He checked his watch and decided that the time had come to go home and see what the rest of the family was up to. And as he got up and started cleaning up a little in anticipation of the cleaning lady coming in later tonight, his phone chimed, and he saw that his wife was trying to reach him.

"Hey, honey," he said. "What's up?"

"Oh, Tex," she said in a teary voice. Immediately he was on high alert.

"What's wrong?"

"Someone has filed a complaint against me with the library authority, and now they've decided to temporarily replace me with a different librarian!"

"What?! What complaint?"

"I don't know. Something about a book I recommended that wasn't age-appropriate. I'm sure I did no such thing, but the person I spoke to said they're taking this very seriously, and for the time being, I can't come to work. Oh, Tex, what am I going to do? If they fire me…"

"They won't fire you," he said immediately. "You're the best librarian this town has ever had. You're devoted to your job and to your library visitors. I'm sure this is all some kind of terrible misunderstanding that will be cleared up in no time."

"I don't know," she said, sniffling a little. "They said I gave a steamy romance book to a young girl and told her to read it from cover to cover. The parents caught it just in time and said it was the most horrible book possible. Pure filth, they called it, and they're threatening to sue the library—and me personally! But I don't remember ever recommending any such book to any young person."

"Like I said, it's probably some misunderstanding," he said. "And the investigation will clear you, and then you can go back to work."

"I hope so," she said. "This library is my life, Tex. Without it, I'm nothing."

"You're not nothing," he stressed. "You're a wife, a mother, a grandmother, and a friend to a lot of people. And we all adore you, honey."

"That's very sweet of you to say," she said. "Well, I guess we'll just have to wait for the results of that inquiry. I asked how long this will take, and they said it might be a couple of weeks. I really don't know what I will do sitting at home for a couple of weeks."

"So why don't you join me here at the office?" he suggested. "You know how your grandmother spends more time away from her desk than actually being present. And I could always use a hand with the patients—it's been busier than usual these past couple of days." He smiled. "And wouldn't it be great to work side by side for a while?"

"Yeah, that would be great," she admitted. "Thanks, Tex. You've cheered me up. I really thought the world was ending when I got this phone call. Quite out of the blue, as well. I don't even remember ever talking to this person, much less recommending this particular book to anyone. It's all so weird."

After he promised to be home soon and hung up, he thought about what a strange time they lived in. One complaint, no matter how erroneous, could mean the end of a career—just like that. He shook his head as he grabbed his bag and headed for the door. And he'd just stepped out and turned the lock when his phone chimed again. This time he didn't recognize the number.

"Tex Poole," he said as he started his short trek home.

"Doctor Poole, this is Eugene Marks with the Office of Professional Medical Conduct for the State of New York. I'm calling to let you know that we've just received a formal complaint against you."

"A complaint?" he said, stunned. Immediately his mind flashed back to Ida Baumgartner's horseshoe-shaped rash. "Are you sure?"

"I'm afraid so. We're obliged by law to follow up on this complaint, and this is an informal notification of same. You'll receive an official notice by post."

"Can I…" He gulped a little. "Can I keep practicing, at least?"

"Oh, absolutely," said the man. "Pending our investigation, you can keep practicing medicine, but I should warn you to make sure that the kind of behavior that the complainant mentioned shouldn't be repeated."

"What… what is the behavior, exactly?" he asked.

"I'm afraid I can't disclose that at this time. But it will all be in the documents you will receive, so that you and your lawyer can prepare yourselves for the hearing."

"There will be a hearing?"

"There is always a hearing, Doctor Poole," said the man patiently. Clearly, he had conducted this same conversation many times before. "So best to be prepared."

"Okay," he said. "So… I shouldn't repeat a certain type of behavior, but you can't tell me what this behavior is?"

"That's exactly right," said the man. "Good day, Doctor Poole."

"Good day," he said.

After the man from the medical board had hung up, he stood there, staring into space for a few moments. It was the first time in his long career that a complaint had been made against him. And even though it had happened to colleagues of his, and he knew that it could always happen to him, it still came as something of a shock. And then all of a sudden his phone started dinging, and when he checked, he saw that his WhatsApp was being inundated with messages from concerned friends and colleagues. At first, he didn't understand what they were going on about, but when he clicked on one of the links they had sent, he saw that a petition campaign had been launched to get his medical license revoked.

As far as he understood, he had made a wrong diagnosis, and his patient had died. Which was very odd, since as far as he could tell, he hadn't lost a patient in quite a while.

CHAPTER 21

*W*e had arrived at Odelia's office, where our human had planned to write an update on this recent spate of cancelations as they were seemingly becoming prevalent in our small town, when a man showed up unannounced and desired to have speech with her. He was a beefy sort of person with a crew cut and a red face. He also wore the same expression on his face Wilbur had been wearing when he had relayed the news that an online campaign had been launched against him. A sort of look of shock and a lack of understanding of what was going on.

"Odelia Kingsley?" he asked as he knocked on the door. "Could I have a word, please?"

"Yes, of course," said Odelia, and told the man to take a seat. She closed her laptop and assumed a listening position. "What can I do for you, Mr…"

"Bearman," he said. "Clint Bearman." For a few moments, he shuffled nervously in his seat, before launching into his story. "I'm getting married this weekend," he announced.

Odelia smiled. "Congratulations. Who's the lucky lady?"

"Well, that's just the thing. She just texted me to let me

know that there won't be a wedding after all. Apparently there's some kind of online story doing the rounds about me that's totally false, I have to stress. And she's read the story and believes everything that's being said about me, and now she's canceled the wedding."

"That's too bad," said Odelia.

"What's even worse—or maybe not, since I really love Cristy and was looking forward to making her my bride—is that I've been fired from my job, and my landlord is kicking me out of my apartment. And all because of these same false rumors that are circulating about me online."

"What rumors?"

He swallowed with difficulty, then darted a look in Dooley and my direction. As usual, we had taken up position in the corner of Odelia's office to have a little nap after the exertions we'd put ourselves through that day. "Well… Maybe I better show you." He took out his phone and placed it on Odelia's desk.

She picked up the phone and frowned as she scrolled through some of the stuff. Finally, she gave him a stern-faced look. "Are you a member of this group, Mr. Beardman? Please tell me the truth. Because if you are, you will understand that I must ask you to leave my office at once."

Dooley and I shared a look of surprise. Usually Odelia isn't so hard on people, so whatever Clint Bearman was being accused of must be very serious indeed.

"I promise you I've never even heard of this group, and I'm definitely not a member. I'm not even sure they exist. It could all be part of this campaign against me."

"Masters of the Universe?" asked Odelia as she handed him back his phone.

"I swear I have nothing to do with them," said Mr. Beardman desperately. "I love pets, I really do. I have a dog at home that I adore. I would never hurt a pet. Never, never,

never. But somehow the whole world now believes I'm some kind of monster."

Odelia's expression softened. "Oddly enough, yours isn't the first case that has come across my desk today. There seems to be some kind of epidemic of these online gossip campaigns that are damaging people's reputations."

"It has certainly damaged mine," said Mr. Beardman. "If the messages I've received so far are true, I'm a social pariah in this town. People deeply, violently, and very vocally hate me. Even my mother called me and told me she'd raised me better than that, and asked me not to show up for her birthday party. It took every bit of persuasiveness to convince her I'm not that person. And even then, I got the impression she didn't fully believe me."

"If what you're saying is true, someone must really have it in for you," said Odelia. "To go to such lengths to create this whole campaign against you."

"I'll say," said Mr. Beardman. "And before you ask, I have absolutely no idea who could possibly be behind this."

"An angry colleague, maybe? An ex-wife?"

"I've never been married before, and before this happened, I got along with all of my colleagues just fine." He shook his head, looking entirely bewildered. "I was hoping that maybe you could shed some light on this? You do have a reputation for being something of a private sleuth in a town that's devoid of private sleuths."

"I'll take a look, if you like," said Odelia. "But what you really should do is file a complaint against these people with the police. A good friend of mine is being targeted in much the same way, and that's what he did."

She didn't mention that her own husband was also being investigated, though it still stood to be seen whether the complaint that had been made against Chase was true or false. It was concerning that Uncle Alec wouldn't even tell us what the complaint was, so we had no way of knowing if it had any merit or not.

"Look, I'll do whatever you want to clear my name," said Mr. Beardman. "And to make things right again with Cristy." He shook his head. "I can't believe my life went off the rails at a moment's notice. When I got up this morning, I was feeling happier than I'd felt in years, knowing that in a few short days I was going to marry the most wonderful woman in the world. And now?" He threw up his hands. "I might as well crawl into a deep hole and wait for the blows to stop coming."

"Do you have a place to stay?"

"I do. My mom is letting me crash in my old bedroom. Though she's not happy about it. All her friends are telling her she should turn me in to the police for animal cruelty. Apparently there are laws against that sort of thing and I could go to jail."

"Your mom won't turn you in, surely," said Odelia.

The man sighed deeply. "I certainly hope not."

CHAPTER 22

*T*ressa was looking forward to her date that evening. By the time she arrived at the restaurant in question, she had gone through all the different iterations of how the evening would progress, ranging from the disastrous to the Disney musical version of her meeting with Douglas. When she finally got there, cooler heads prevailed, and she figured she and the talented barista would simply share a nice meal and have a good time. Everything that happened after that she would consider a pleasant bonus. What she hadn't reckoned on, though, was that when Douglas finally showed up he wouldn't look as cheerful as he had done when he had delivered that 'Douglas Special' but seemed oddly distant and absentminded.

"Hey, Tressa," he said when he came walking up to her, dressed in a snazzy black leather jacket and ripped jeans. He gave her a quick peck on the cheek, which sent a frisson of excitement traveling up her spine and elicited butterflies in her belly, and then held the door for her as they entered the place he had selected.

All through the preliminary stages of dinner, he kept

glancing at his phone, which he had placed next to his plate, and she was starting to suspect that the evening might not go as she had envisioned. He didn't even seem all that interested in the stories she told about herself and her job, after he had asked her a few perfunctory questions, then became absent-minded again as she talked.

"Tell me about you," she finally invited. "I've been doing all the talking so far."

"Oh, there isn't a lot to tell, to be honest," said Douglas, which she knew couldn't possibly be true, since he seemed to be about the most interesting man she had ever met. "I own a small coffee shop and in my spare time I paint a little—nothing special."

"You're a painter?" she asked.

But he was involved in his phone again, and by the time she looked up, the entrees had arrived and as she tasted the delicious risotto, she noticed how he almost didn't touch his food.

"It's delicious," she said.

"Mh," he said.

She couldn't understand it. That morning he'd been all charm and friendliness, and also when he had unexpectedly shown up at work. And now it seemed as if he'd rather be anywhere but with her. It saddened her, and upset her more than she had expected. Clearly, she had read too much into his intentions.

They ate the rest of their entrees in silence, and by the time the spaghetti arrived, she wished the meal was at an end already and she could go home. Her self-esteem might not be all that great, but it certainly told her she deserved better than this.

Suddenly his phone dinged, and he shot up as if stung. "I'm sorry, but I have to take this," he murmured, then got up from the table and disappeared for five minutes. When he returned, he looked even worse than before.

"What's wrong?" she asked.

"Mh? Oh, nothing."

"It doesn't look like it's nothing," she said, determined to get to the bottom of this. He was the one who had invited her, and he was behaving like a jerk.

He was silent for a moment, then gave her a pained look. "I know I haven't been the best company tonight, and I'm sorry. It's just that..."

"Yes?" She was still willing to give him the benefit of the doubt.

"It's my sister," he said. "She's pregnant, and there has been a complication."

Immediately, her heart went out to him. "Oh, that's terrible. Is she in the hospital?"

He nodded. "She is. Her husband is keeping the rest of the family informed, but it doesn't look good. It's possible that she might lose the baby."

"Oh, Douglas, I'm so sorry," she said, immediately feeling like a jerk herself for judging him so harshly. Of course, if his sister was going through a horrible thing like that, he couldn't be expected to be great company. "Maybe you should go and be with her," she suggested. "We can have dinner some other time."

He gave her a hopeful look. "Are you sure? I didn't want to cancel, but this whole thing with my sister is keeping me from enjoying our time together."

"Absolutely," she said. "You don't even have to ask."

Immediately, he threw down his napkin and got up. "I'll pay for dinner, of course. And I'll call you." And before she could say anything, he was gone.

It was so abrupt she wondered if she had let him off the hook too easily. But then she chided herself for being cold-hearted and cruel. The guy's sister might lose her baby. And here she was feeling sorry for herself. And so she ate the rest of her meal, even though the food didn't taste as good as before Douglas had left. And as she sat there taking a sip from her wine, she decided to send him a message. Something sweet and caring to show him she understood.

But as she picked up her phone, she saw that Bonnie had tried to get in touch with her. She opened the message and saw it contained a link to an online petition campaign. And as she checked the page, for a moment she didn't understand what she was seeing. The headline read, 'My life with a love cheat.' And as she scanned through the text, she soon saw that the love cheat was Douglas. If what this person had written was true, he had dated this girl, gotten her pregnant, and had then left her. Later she had discovered that he had cheated on her with her best friend and had gotten her pregnant also. The petition called for Douglas's coffee shop to be boycotted and to warn other women against the man.

As she put down her phone, she realized she'd had a narrow escape.

CHAPTER 23

That evening, the mood around the dinner table was a little subdued, I have to say. The family had come together at Odelia and Chase's home, where the latter had arranged to treat them to his famous spaghetti bolognese. I'm not sure what had gone wrong, but apparently the taste of the cop's meatballs was off this time, but even though everyone soldiered on regardless, pretending everything was fine, it wasn't the feast it usually was. At one point, Uncle Alec tried to feed us his meatballs under the table, but even though we had a little taste, our infallible instinct told us to desist, and so the rest of the meatballs were left untouched.

By the time the meal ended, the floor was littered with meatballs, with no takers.

"There's something wrong with Chase's meatballs," Brutus said.

"Not just his meatballs," said Harriet. "He looks sad."

"That's because he's suspended," I said. "It's not a lot of fun being suspended when you love your job. Especially when your boss refuses to give you a reason."

All throughout dinner, conversation had centered on

114

every possible topic except Chase's recent suspension, which was understandable, since both the suspender and the suspendee, so to speak, were sitting right next to one another. And since Uncle Alec had made it clear he wasn't allowed to divulge the exact reason for the suspension, the atmosphere was fraught with a certain tension.

Finally, Marge couldn't hold it any longer. "Just tell us what it is," she begged her brother. "We're all family around this table, and nobody is going to blab about what you reveal to us in confidence. So just tell us already, Alec."

"Yeah, what is it that I did?" asked Chase, still giving us a very accurate portrayal of a kicked puppy.

Uncle Alec exchanged a look with Charlene, who finally gave him the nod. The police chief looked relieved. "A complaint has been made," he explained. "And it goes right to your character, which is why we have to be careful how to proceed."

"My character? What do you mean?" asked Chase.

The Chief shook his head. "You gave a false statement. Basically, you lied, and obviously we can't have that."

"Lied about what?" asked Odelia.

"There was an incident with a fellow officer, where you and he visited the home of a suspect. You questioned the suspect, who gave his version of events, but then later when the officer checked the record, you had given an entirely different account of the suspect's words. To the effect that it showed him as innocent when it was obvious to the officer that he was guilty of the facts he was accused of."

Chase looked so bewildered it was almost funny. "I don't get it," he confessed. "What suspect? What fellow officer? I really don't recall any such incident."

Uncle Alec gave him a strange look. "You were there, Chase. I've got the incident report, your statement, the statement of the fellow officer, the whole deal. And I have to say there are discrepancies."

"Discrepancies? What discrepancies?"

"The suspect, a low-level drug dealer, admitted to the facts he was being accused of. Only according to your report, he denied the whole thing. Now the allegation being made against you is that you accepted a bribe in exchange for letting the guy off the hook."

"A bribe!" Chase cried. "But I would never—"

Uncle Alec held up his hand. "This is exactly why I didn't want to tell you. These things are best handled by an independent inquiry, not at the dinner table."

"But I swear I wasn't even there! The last time I interrogated a drug dealer must be months ago." He narrowed his eyes. "Who's the fellow officer?"

"Can't tell you," said the Chief curtly.

"Who's the suspect?"

But the Chief shook his head.

"Uncle Alec, you know as well as I do that Chase would never take a bribe," Odelia argued.

"We all suffer from moments of weakness," said her uncle. "And we're all tempted at such times. So it's not unreasonable to suppose—"

"But it *is* unreasonable!" said Chase. "I've never taken a bribe in my life!"

"I'm afraid it's your word against that of your fellow officer," said the Chief.

Marge and Tex, who had kept very quiet throughout this back-and-forth, now cleared their throats. "There's something we think you should know," said Marge. "I've been suspended from the library for the time being. And your father is being investigated by the medical board. So it looks as if Chase isn't the only one in this family who's in trouble right now."

"This whole town is going to hell in a handbasket," said Gran with customary brevity. "Even Wilbur, of all people, is under suspicion. If this keeps up *I'll* be suspended—not sure from what, though I guess they'll find something to suspend me from. The senior center, maybe. Persona non grata. And Scarlett, too." She wagged a finger at Charlene. "Watch your back, little lady. Cause before you know it, one of your political opponents will launch a smear campaign against you!"

"I'm sure it won't come to that," Charlene assured her mother-in-law.

"Oh, I wouldn't be so sure about that. There's a virus raging in this town, and it's attacking all of us." She turned to Odelia. "Tell them about that poor sap who turned up in your office this afternoon. Cut loose by his fiancée, fired from his job, and kicked out by his landlord. And for what? Because of some nasty rumors."

"It's true," Odelia confirmed. "There seems to be a whole wave of this thing. Remember Garret Root?"

"Another case I'm not allowed to touch," Chase muttered, giving Uncle Alec a nasty look, which caused the older man to sag a little in response.

"Or the spiked cookies," Gran reminded us. "That may also be bogus."

"Do you think these instances of people being investigated are all connected somehow?" asked Charlene.

"I don't know," said Odelia. "But it's too much of a coincidence that this all happens at the same time, wouldn't you say? Even in our own family three people are under suspicion. That smells fishy to me."

Dooley looked up at this. "Fish?" he asked. "Where?"

Clearly Chase's meatballs hadn't satisfied his craving for something delicious.

"I'm going to dig a little deeper into this tomorrow,"

Odelia promised. "See what I can find out." She turned to the four of us. "And I hope I can count on your participation."

"Absolutely," I said.

"You can count on us," said Brutus.

"We'll leave no stone unturned," said Harriet.

"I don't smell fish," said Dooley fervently. "And I have a really good nose, so if there was any fish, I would have smelled it by now."

CHAPTER 24

Dinner had ended, and everyone got busy clearing the plates and loading the dishwasher when the doorbell rang out its pleasant but insistent sound. When Odelia returned moments later, it was with Wilbur Vickery and Kingman in tow. Neither of them looked entirely happy with life.

"Vandals have taken over the store," the shop owner lamented. "They've ransacked the place and stolen the most valuable items like liquor and cigarettes. The police arrived after I called it in, and they've locked down the place for now, but frankly, I don't feel safe anymore." He gave Odelia a searching look. "So I wanted to ask if I could possibly crash at your place for the time being? Until this whole harassment campaign dies down again?"

"They called me names," Kingman intimated. "Names I won't repeat."

I now saw that something had been spray-painted on his coat. "What's that?" I asked.

"Oh, it's nothing," said Kingman, clearly embarrassed about the addition to his fine coat. "Some louts managed to hit me with it. I'm sure they meant to hit Wilbur, but I ended up receiving the brunt of their attack."

"This is really getting out of hand," said Uncle Alec. "If this continues, there will be riots in the street next." He was addressing himself at Charlene, whose frown indicated that she took his words very seriously indeed.

"We need to stop these campaigns before the whole town gets riled up," she agreed. "But how? We can't shut down the entire internet—that's impossible."

"You have to call an emergency meeting of the town council," Uncle Alec advised. "And make sure our local business community is protected from these vandals. If not checked, this type of violence can quickly escalate and spread."

Charlene nodded. "You're absolutely right. I'll call for an emergency meeting first thing tomorrow morning."

"Of course you can stay," said Gran as she patted Wilbur on the back. "In fact, you can stay for as long as you like. Odelia and Chase have a perfectly accommodating spare bedroom available just for you. Isn't that so, honey?"

Odelia didn't look entirely convinced, but since she's a human being with a big heart, she nodded in acquiescence. "I'll show you the room," she said. "It's a little messy right now, but we'll get you installed in no time." And as she led him up the stairs, we heard her ask, "They didn't hurt you, did they, these vandals?"

"They threw something at me, but I ducked," he said. "I think they got Kingman, though."

"They did," Kingman confirmed. "Good thing I'm built like a rock."

I would have said he was more built like a very sizable and very comfortable pillow, but I wisely kept my tongue. The poor cat had been through enough for one night.

"We need to do something about this," said Harriet. "First

Kingman is canceled, and now he's being attacked. This can't go on, Max."

"No, there must be something we can do," Brutus added.

"It's not fair that Kingman is chased out of his own home," I agreed.

"Did you have to leave your lute behind, Kingman?" asked Dooley.

Kingman gave him a strange look but decided not to engage. "If you could talk to Shanille and ask if I can have my place in cat choir back, that would go a long way to restoring my equanimity. She seems to believe I'm some kind of monster, but I can assure you that I'm not, you guys."

"We know you're not a monster, Kingman," I said.

And so it was decided: we'd go to the park and reason with Shanille and plead with cat choir's conductor to allow Kingman back in the choir. And then we'd try and find out who had started this campaign against our friend and why. In the meantime, Odelia would give Wilbur a bed for the night and protect him from the rabid mob that seemed intent on putting him out of business.

"Scarlett and I will patrol the streets tonight, if you want," Gran suggested. "To make sure that no more violence is perpetrated."

"And how are you going to contend with a violent mob?" Uncle Alec asked. "I'd much rather you stayed home, Ma. I don't want to see you getting hurt."

"Fine," said the old lady, holding up her hands. "Whatever you say."

We left the house via the backyard, and moments later were en route to the park. Kingman seemed hesitant to join us, claiming he'd been banned from the park and he didn't want to risk breaking the ban.

"It will be fine," Harriet assured him. "Shanille may be a

lot of things, but she's not unreasonable. The moment we explain things to her, she will understand."

It didn't take us long to arrive at the park, but as we entered via the main entrance, who did we see but Shanille herself? She was licking what looked like a scratch across her nose, and when we joined her, she gave us a sad look. "I've been canceled, you guys. Can you believe it? Me! Cat choir's very own director!"

"But why?" I asked, much perturbed. "And by who?"

"A couple of sopranos. They claimed I'm too overbearing, and too dictatorial, and they're going to organize cat choir along lines of radical democracy from now on, which means it won't have an actual conductor anymore."

"But then who's going to lead it?" asked Harriet, as stunned as we all were.

"No one!" said Shanille. "That's the thing. They're taking cat choir in a new direction. No more leaders, no more conductors. The members will take charge." Harriet clearly didn't believe in this novel concept, for she kept asking how this would work. But Shanille shrugged her shoulders. "I don't know and frankly I don't care. After they canceled me, they also kicked me out and told me never to return. Looks like my days as cat choir's conductor are effectively over."

"Oh, but that's so sad," said Dooley. "And Kingman here was just learning how to play the lute. That would have been such a fine addition to the choir."

Shanille gave Kingman a measured look. "I thought I told you to stay away from me? Does the concept 'restraining order' mean nothing to you, Kingman?"

The large cat gave me a hopeful look, and so I cleared my throat. "I think there's been some kind of misunderstanding. Kingman swears up and down that he never put a paw wrong, and that this whole business with the lewd behavior is a rumor started by cats who have it in for him. In other words, it's all bogus."

Shanille considered this. "Oddly enough, the same cats that have canceled me are also the ones who made that initial complaint about Kingman, so maybe there is some truth to what you're saying, Max."

"Of course there's truth to what Max is saying," said Harriet. "If Kingman really were a sex pest, do you think I wouldn't have noticed? I'm the prettiest cat in all of Hampton Cove, so if he really were that cat, I would have been first on his list of cats to hit on. The fact that I've never experienced anything of the kind means he's innocent."

"It's possible," said Shanille, as she studied Kingman, trying to determine if he really was a sex pest or not. Then she spotted the paint on his coat. "What's that?"

"Wilbur's store is being targeted by a group of vandals," said Kingman. "And I got caught in the crossfire."

This seemed to cinch things, for her expression turned solicitous. "I'm so sorry, Kingman, for what I've put you through. I should have remembered that old standby of innocent until proven guilty. And to be totally honest, I've never experienced any of that kind of behavior from you either, so…" She frowned. "I wonder what their motive was for casting you out. You must have done something to upset them, or otherwise they wouldn't be singling you out."

"Who made that complaint about Kingman?" I asked.

"Kitty and Musti," she said, referring to two newish members of cat choir.

"I'm friends with Musti," said Harriet. "I'll talk to her, if you like."

"Could you?" Shanille asked. "And find out what they plan to do with cat choir?" She gave us a mournful look. "That choir is my life's work, after all."

She was clearly sad to let it go, which was understandable.

"I'll go and talk to her now," said Harriet. She turned to the rest of us. "Are you coming? Except you, Kingman. And you, Shanille. Apparently you're both persona non grata now." Somehow, she seemed to derive a certain pleasure out of saying these words. Though I could have been mistaken, of course.

As it was, Kingman and Shanille stayed behind, while we launched into our new mission of finding out what was going on with cat choir.

CHAPTER 25

*G*arret Root gazed out of the window of his brother Jim's kitchen at the full moon that had hoisted itself up onto the horizon and seemed determined to remain there for the time being. He had to admit that he was having mixed feelings about his present surroundings. On the one hand, he was grateful for the respite, but on the other, he wasn't sure that hiding away from the big bad world out there was the best course of action going forward. After all, at some point, he would have to face his accusers and the terrible things they were accusing him of.

He looked up when his sister Cristy walked into the kitchen carrying the dirty plates she had collected from the dinner table. "And how are you holding up?" she asked.

"Oh, as well as can be expected," he said. "I've switched off my phone, so it's easy to pretend that nothing is going on." He studied her face and saw she looked as pale and drawn as she had all evening. "How are things with you?"

She grimaced. "As if someone stuck his hand in my insides and gave it a good rummage." She sighed deeply. "As if this whole business with Clint isn't enough to deal with, now I've got caterers and wedding planners and dozens of guests to handle. If you thought that organizing the actual wedding is a pain in the patootie, trying to cancel one a couple of days before the event isn't much easier, let me tell you." She gave him a look of commiseration. "Look at us. Both being put through the wringer."

"At least Mom and Dad seem to be taking it pretty well," he said. They had all been concerned that their elderly parents would be adversely affected by the news that their daughter's wedding was canceled and that their son was being accused of all kinds of things.

"Yeah, I'm surprised, actually. Especially by Mom's reaction. She seemed almost resigned. As if she'd been expecting something like this."

"I think they're both putting up a front," said Garret. "No way are they all right with this, but what else can they say? They can see we're suffering agonies."

Jim now walked into the kitchen, looking chipper and bright as usual. He rubbed his hands. "So let's put dessert on the table."

"Look at you being all bright and bushy-tailed," said Cristy with a touch of annoyance.

"I'm sorry," said Jim. "But business is booming, all of a sudden."

"So that big client you were hoping to land finally came through?" asked Cristy.

"He did," said Jim. "And if things go as planned, he's promised to send a lot more business my way. It's all about stepping stones, you guys. Stepping stones to greater success." But then he seemed to realize who he was talking to, for he put a damper on the exuberance. "Mom and Dad told me they're very concerned about you two, but they know that somehow everything will be all right in the end."

"Garret and I were just saying how surprised we are that

they're taking it so well," said Cristy. "Especially Mom, who, you have to admit, is something of a worrywart."

"I told her before they arrived what was going on," Jim confessed. "I didn't want her to be unprepared going in."

"What did you tell her, exactly?" asked Cristy, crossing her arms in front of her chest.

"Oh, just the basic facts," Jim assured her. "That there won't be a wedding after you found out certain things about the groom that made him unsuitable as your future husband. And that a colleague at Garret's school has made certain wrongful allegations against him, but that you're working with the school to have it all cleared up in no time."

"We'll have to see about that," said Garret. He had a feeling that nothing would be cleared up any time soon. At least if Principal Hollins's words were any indication. The last time he had spoken to her, her exact words were, 'Your career is over, Root,' or words to that effect. And her inflection hadn't been encouraging, or the way she had hung up on him when he had questioned her further.

No, if he ever returned to the teaching profession, it wouldn't be at Gordon Jovitt, or any local school, for that matter. In fact, he got the impression he might never stand in front of a classroom again.

And it was either a testament to his resilience or his naiveté that he hadn't collapsed into a heap and succumbed to a feeling of extreme depression. Sometimes he thought that the only thing that kept him going was the knowledge that Odelia Kingsley had his case well in hand. And as his brother and sister returned to the living room with dessert, he took out his phone and googled Odelia Kingsley. Great was his surprise when he discovered that she wasn't a wizened old lady with white curly hair but a young woman of attractive aspect.

He frowned as he studied her picture. So who had the

Odelia Kingsley been that he had talked to that morning? More importantly, who was working on his case right now? And as he looked up with a frown of concern, he suddenly noticed that one member of the family was conspicuously absent from the festivities being organized in Jim's living room.

It was Susan, and try as he might, he couldn't locate the beagle anywhere.

The only thing he could think of was that he had returned home.

CHAPTER 26

*I*t wasn't long before we arrived at the playground, which is the preferred location for cat choir's nightly rehearsals. Only there wasn't a lot of singing going on. Cats just stood haphazardly spread out across the playground's different fixtures and structures, such as there are: the swing, the slide, the seesaw, the carousel, the sandpit, the jungle gym, and the trampoline. All of them seemed to be having a whale of a time, with laughter ringing out at regular intervals, and plenty of chatter taking place.

"Why aren't you rehearsing?" asked Harriet of the first cat we encountered. It was Buster, who belongs to our local barber and hair stylist.

"Oh, that's all a thing of the past," Buster assured us. "There will be no more singing. In fact, cat choir has been abolished."

"But… I thought that someone else was taking over from Shanille?" asked Harriet.

"No one is taking over," said Buster.

One of our other friends now joined the conversation. It was Tigger, who belonged to the plumber. "Isn't this a lot more fun?" he said. "No more Shanille means no more telling us what to do and when to do it! I have to say I love it."

"But the whole purpose of cat choir is to sing," said Harriet.

"I think you'll find that was Shanille's project," said Buster. "But now that she's gone, we can simply hang out and do whatever we want. No more dictator!"

"I thought she did a pretty good job," I said. "Keeping everyone in line, I mean."

"That's exactly the point, Max," said Buster. "Why do we need anyone to keep us in line? That's such an old-fashioned concept. I, for one, think it's much better this way." He gestured to the other members of the former cat choir with an all-encompassing gesture of his paw. "Just look around you. Nothing but happy faces. We're all relieved to finally be free from Shanille's tyrannical rule."

"He's right," said Tigger. "Free at last. Hurray for freedom!"

Harriet's face fell. "But… how am I going to sing my solos?"

Buster and Tigger shared a grin. "No more solos, Harriet," said Buster.

"Never again!" Tigger added, and I got the feeling that Harriet's solos wouldn't exactly be missed.

I had been looking around in search of Musti and Kitty and finally located the dynamic duo. And since I was determined to get to the bottom of this business of getting rid of Shanille, I set paw in their direction. By the time I got there, they had already been alerted to my arrival, for they gave me a scrutinizing look.

"Well, look who's here," said Musti, a dark-haired petite feline. "If it isn't Hampton Cove's great detective." Somehow I got the impression she was being ironic, but I didn't let that deter me from saying what I had to say.

"Is it true that you told Shanille never to return to the park?" I asked.

"And what if we did?" asked her friend Kitty. She was a feline of a more butch aspect, with a coat that was a mixture of blond and white. "When we arrived in town we immediately surmised that cats weren't happy with the iron yoke that Shanille had placed on their necks. So we set out to free them from that yoke."

"You have to admit that Shanille is something of a tyrant, Max," said Musti. "Always telling other cats what to do, and throwing her weight around. We both thought it was time to put an end to that."

"The time of the tyrant is over," said Kitty. "We're free now, so let's enjoy that."

"Well, it's true that Shanille can be strict," I admitted. "But only because she wants us to perform to the best of our abilities. And the only way to run a choir is to take things in paw and impose a certain discipline. How else are dozens of cats ever going to sing as one voice and achieve harmony?"

But Kitty and Musti would have none of this. "Nonsense, Max," said Musti. "Shanille has obviously done a number on you."

"She's been gaslighting you," Kitty added. "Making you think that her way is the only way when it's not. I mean, look at all of those happy faces, Max. They're all relieved that the witch is dead, and that they can finally do what they enjoy."

I looked around, and even though I did see a lot of happy faces, I didn't hear any of the fine harmonies cat choir sometimes achieved under the tutelage of Shanille. We didn't always sound the way we should, but working toward a common goal was still a fine achievement that went a long way to establishing a sense of purpose and community spirit.

"But... they're just talking," I said. "They're not singing."

Musti and Kitty both laughed. "Welcome to the new world, Max."

"Looks like Max's little mind is blown," said Musti in a mocking tone.

"You have to keep up with the times, Maxie!" said Kitty. "Or be left behind."

Harriet now came stalking up, looking out of sorts. "How am I supposed to sing my solos now?" she demanded. "And who's actually in charge here?"

"This may surprise you, Harriet," said Musti with a touch of hauteur. "But there's more to life than singing solos, you know. And as for who's in charge: no one. Since cat choir has ceased to exist."

Harriet's jaw dropped. "What? No more cat choir?"

Kitty grinned mischievously. "No more cat choir."

"But you can't do that!" said Harriet.

"Watch us," said Musti. Then she shouted at the top of her lungs. "Does anyone of you want cat choir to continue?"

Out of the throats of dozens of cats, one word sounded: "Noooooo!"

Kitty held up her paws. "See? Better get used to it, Harriet. Cat choir is canceled."

CHAPTER 27

"What about Kingman?" asked Harriet. "Has he been canceled, too?"

Kitty gave her a keen look. "Watch your step, Harriet," she said. "Pretty soon I'll be led to conclude that you're carrying a torch for that sex pest."

Harriet bridled. "But Kingman is no sex pest. He's our friend!"

Musti stiffened. "Then I'm afraid you have no place here anymore."

"Yeah," Kitty agreed. "We don't condone that kind of behavior, and we certainly don't condone apologists of any kind."

"But what did he do to you?" I asked.

"He called me a lewd name, and I don't appreciate that kind of talk. And since then I've heard from many other females that Kingman is known for this."

"What surprises me is why you've tolerated him for so long," said Musti. "If I didn't know any better, I'd say you're covering for him. Which makes you just as bad as he is." She shook her head decidedly. "Male chauvinism is a thing of the past and has no place in our midst. So Kingman is gone. And since we don't tolerate tyrannical behavior either, Shanille is out as well." She then gave me a threatening look. "And if you two don't get with the program, you will both find yourselves on the wrong side of history, just like Kingman and Shanille."

"You don't want to antagonize us, Max," Kitty warned.

"Or you, Harriet," Musti added.

Harriet gulped and seemed shocked by these words. But when she gave me a searching look, I shook my head. Best not to go against this duo. It could only lead to more trouble. And so I plastered my most gracious smile onto my face and said, "We wouldn't *think* of antagonizing you. Isn't that right, Harriet?"

Harriet nodded three times in quick succession. "That's right," she said in a strangled voice. And then quickly walked away, clearly not trusting herself with these two cats.

"Good cat, Max," said Musti as she patted me on the head in a sort of patronizing way. "It takes intelligence to know which way the wind blows."

"I think Max can sense that the reign of the likes of Kingman and Shanille is over," said Kitty, eyeing me closely. "And the same goes for all of their friends."

"Cronyism is a thing of the past," Musti professed. "And Max knows this."

"I do," I assured them. "And I think it's admirable the way you're heralding in such an exciting new chapter in the history of Hampton Cove's cat population. A fresh breeze to waft through this town. Out with the old, in with the new."

Both Musti and Kitty nodded with satisfaction. "He gets it," said Musti.

"He really does," Kitty confirmed.

"You can stay, Max."

I guess I just got paid the highest compliment a cat could

be paid in this new constellation of things. A constellation where Musti and Kitty were the new rulers of the roost. At least I hadn't been canceled. For now.

I returned to my friends, who all looked as discombobulated as I was feeling. And since we felt we didn't really have a place in this new cat choir that wasn't even a choir anymore, we walked away. On our way, we passed dog choir, and it was with a touch of chagrin mingled with regret that Harriet said, "At least they still get to sing." Then she got an idea. "Maybe we should join dog choir?"

But as we sat and watched, it soon became clear that dog choir wasn't much of a choir. They whimpered, they yelped, they groaned and grunted and whined and howled, but none of it was exactly in sync. I think what they lacked was a firm paw to bring everything together. Which is when Harriet stepped to the fore.

"If you like, we could teach you how to sing in harmony. You can even benefit from the greatest conductor the world has ever known." For a moment I thought she was going to place a paw to her chest and exclaim, 'Moi!' But instead she smiled and said, "Shanille is an extremely talented and dedicated conductor, and since she's currently between jobs, she might be induced to take dog choir in hand and turn you into the best dog choir in the land."

The members of dog choir, who had stopped their concert, stared at the Persian with interest. Then Rufus, our neighbors' sheepdog, piped up, "Shanille would be willing to be our conductor?"

"Absolutely," Harriet assured him.

Fifi, our other neighbor's Yorkie, gave the Persian a look of hope. "We could really use a professional. Wouldn't you agree, you guys?"

The other dogs, all friends of ours, agreed wholeheartedly. And so it was decided. We'd lobby with Shanille to take over dog choir, since cat choir had dispensed with her services. And since the rest of us had nowhere to go, we all decided then and there to join dog choir and turn it into a mixed-species choir instead.

Harriet hurried off to fetch Shanille and Kingman, and Dooley, Brutus, and myself took up positions among the dogs. They didn't seem to be aware of the distinction between the different parts, so we told them all about bass, tenor, soprano, and alto. Before long, animated conversation was being conducted, and a new excitement galvanized our fellow pets into a sort of frenzied chatter.

That all ended when Shanille came walking up. True to form, the disgraced and canceled conductor asserted her customary brand of authority, and before long was turning this ragtag group of cats and dogs into an actual choir. The moment Harriet sang her first solo of the night, accompanied by a tiny Poodle to sing harmonies, we all got the chills.

Which is when the first shoe hit, causing all the dogs to cheer.

"We never get any shoes thrown at us!" Rufus explained.

"It's a badge of honor," Fifi added happily.

And as we launched into our second song of the night, I saw a dog move amongst the nearby trees, reluctant to approach. I recognized him as Susan, Garret Root's beagle. And so as Shanille explained the ins and outs of what constitutes a great song, I hurried over to the beagle.

"Why don't you join us?" I suggested.

"I've actually come to talk to you, Max," he said. "Have you found out what's going on with this cancel business? Will Garret be able to go back to work soon?"

Which is when I sadly had to inform him that we hadn't found out a lot. Only that Garret wasn't the only one who was being canceled in Hampton Cove.

"In fact, it looks as if Garret will soon be part of the

majority instead of the minority," I told the beagle. "More and more people are being canceled. Pretty soon, there won't be anyone left to cancel but the people doing the canceling!"

It wasn't exactly the message he had been hoping for, but it still bucked him up to some extent. And as he joined the lineup, very soon he proved himself to be a very serviceable bass singer. Which is when Harriet suggested changing the name of the choir from dog choir to 'the choir of the canceled.'

It seemed as good a name as any, and it certainly reflected an aspect of the truth, even though for the moment some of us had escaped this dreaded fate.

Though I had a feeling that it wouldn't be long before Harriet, Dooley, Brutus, and myself would also be canceled and join the ranks of those countless others.

CHAPTER 28

The next morning, bright and early, we were all present in Odelia's office for a meeting that would determine the future of Hampton Cove, or so Gran had announced. Odelia was there, of course, but also Chase, Odelia's mom and dad, her grandmother, Scarlett, Wilbur Vickery, and about a dozen other people who had been 'canceled.' I recognized Garret Root, Clint Bearman, and several others I'd never seen before, but who all looked a little dejected, I had to say. Which wasn't surprising when the first person got up and cleared his throat.

"My name is Douglas Lawler," he said, "and I've been canceled." He took a deep breath. "I work as a barista in my own coffee shop, but I didn't even bother to open the shop this morning as late last night rumors started circulating online about certain unacceptable behavior on my part. I'd asked a woman out on a date, but even before I arrived, I saw that a petition had been launched to demand an investigation into my so-called transgressions. Suffice it to say, I felt obliged to cut the date short as I didn't want to burden the woman with my problems."

"What did she say about the allegations?" asked Odelia.

"I don't know. I made some excuse about my sister being at the hospital, and I fled," said the man.

He was a man of exceedingly handsome aspect, with bronzed features and slicked-back dark hair, and I got the impression that he was the type of man women would swoon over. The frown of concern etched on his brow also told me that his personal appearance was the least of his worries right now.

The humans present were all sitting in a circle in Odelia's office, with our human acting as chairperson.

"My name is Garret Root," said Garret as he got up. "And I've been canceled. I've lost my job, my reputation, and my life has been ruined. And I don't even know why."

And so on and on it went, with person after person taking the proverbial stage and telling us how this recent plague sweeping our town had affected them.

"I'm Kingman, and I've also been canceled," Kingman said at a certain point, right after Wilbur had given us his story, but I don't think anyone paid him any attention. We did though, and assured him that he may have been canceled by some, but certainly not by us.

Chase then organized a round of questions to determine if there were any commonalities between the different participants, apart from the fact that they all had their lives wrecked by a person or persons unknown. But try as he might, he couldn't really nail down any particular thing they all had in common. Garret was a schoolteacher, Clint worked in insurance, Douglas owned his own coffee shop. And none of the three men knew each other socially, even though Garret and Clint had at one time frequented Douglas's coffee shop the Happy Bean. But then a lot of the others present had, and then some of them hadn't. And then there were Wilbur and Chase, who were as different as they could have been. One a detective, the other the owner of the General Store. At first glance, they had nothing in common. And even when Gran pointed out they were both in law enforcement, Chase in an official capacity and Wilbur as a member of her neighborhood watch, that didn't make a big impression either.

"This can't be a coordinated campaign, can it?" asked Clint. "I mean, the fact that all of us are being targeted must be a coincidence, right?"

"I wouldn't be so sure about that," said Chase. "Though it looks like none of us have anything in common, it still feels off to me that we're all in the same boat."

"These complaints all seem to share the same hallmarks," Odelia agreed. "There's a rumor being started online and shared on social media, a petition campaign demanding action from the authorities, requests for contracts being terminated, people being thrown out of their apartments, shunned by their friends and their local community. I mean, there's definitely a pattern here."

"Can we really say that we're all innocent, though?" asked Garret. "I mean, I know I'm innocent—mostly."

"What do you mean, mostly?" asked Gran.

"Well, I'm being accused of exposing myself to some of the kids in my school, right? And that part is absolutely false. That never happened. But Odelia told me that a teacher told her I tried to kiss her at a Christmas party, and that's true. I did try to kiss her. Thing is, I thought at the time she wanted to be kissed. Turns out that wasn't the case, so in that sense I'm guilty."

"But Melody's story wasn't part of the original complaint made against you," Chase pointed out. "She only added that when she learned of the other stuff."

"True," Garret admitted. "But that still doesn't make me innocent." He looked around at the other participants. "Who of you can say they're without blame?" Hands were hesitantly raised, until all of them were in the air, and Garret nodded. "Okay, forget what I said. Obviously, my comment was ill-placed."

"No, I think you may be onto something," said Chase. "All of us have done stuff that we're not proud of, but that's nothing compared to what we're being accused of. It does make us feel that maybe there is some truth to the rumors."

"I know that I've flirted with several of my customers," said Douglas. "But I definitely never assaulted anyone, as this campaign will have you believe."

"I never hurt a pet," said Clint. "But I did once pull my cat's tail. In my defense, I was five at the time, and I didn't pull very hard."

Smiles lit up faces all around the room, and as other participants told of some of their transgressions, it soon became clear they were a far cry from what they were currently being accused of, which were acts punishable by law, to say the least.

"Another aspect of these campaigns that I've noticed," said Odelia, "is that all of the accusers wish to remain anonymous. I mean, no one has actually come forward and filed an actual complaint with the police."

"My fiancée filed a complaint," said Clint. "Not that she ever saw me hurt a pet, but she saw the stories being circulated online and wanted to make sure I wasn't getting away with it." His face sagged. "She even sent me a copy of the complaint. So instead of a wedding certificate, I got an official complaint."

"Look, I think we all agree that something very suspicious is going on," said Chase, leaning forward. "Unfortunately, I've been suspended from active duty, so I can't officially investigate any of this. But I will promise you one thing: my wife and I will do our level best to get to the bottom of this phenomenon."

"And so will the neighborhood watch," Gran added for good measure.

"And until we do, my advice to you is to lay low," Odelia said. "And not to give these people more ammunition to hurt you with."

"I'm staying with my brother," said Garret.

"I'm staying with my parents," said Clint.

"I'm staying with a friend," said Douglas.

"I'm staying with Odelia and Chase," said Wilbur.

"And I'm staying with Max and Dooley," said Kingman, giving us a grateful look.

"And you can stay as long as you like," I told our friend.

"In the meantime, let's keep meeting like this," Odelia suggested.

"What are we going to call ourselves?" asked Garret.

Chase grinned. "How about Canceled Anonymous?"

With a show of hands, his suggestion was unanimously accepted, and so a new organization was born. The members of the CA would meet every week in Odelia's office from now on and until this whole sordid matter was resolved.

CHAPTER 29

*A*fter the inaugural meeting of Canceled Anonymous was over, Odelia and Chase organized a meeting of their own. Now that Chase didn't have a job to go to anymore, he might as well get to the bottom of what was going on.

"Has your colleague talked to Natalie Francis yet?" asked Odelia, referring to the interview she and Chase were going to conduct the previous day until Chase had been suspended and replaced by a younger model.

"Yeah, I asked your uncle about it last night, and he said it was a bust. Natalie Francis swears up and down that she never put any illegal substances in her cookies, and if anyone says otherwise she's ready to sue. Why? Do you think there's a connection with any of this cancel business?"

Odelia shook her head. "I don't know. Just following up on what turned out to be my last official case as a civilian consultant." She sighed. "We had a great run, didn't we, babe?"

"We sure did," said Chase. "And I sincerely hope it's goodbye for now, not forever."

They were both quiet for a moment, then started listing all the different victims of this cancel campaign sweeping through our town and trying to come up with possible links that could tie them all together. But try as they might, they couldn't see it, and frankly neither could I. And so after listening to them knock their heads against the wall, I decided to step out of the office for a moment to get some fresh air—and some perspective.

And so the four of us left the office and went for a little walk to clear our heads.

"This is all very baffling," said Harriet. "But what if—and bear with me here for a moment—what if there *is* no connection? What if all these accusations are real? I mean, we all know that Wilbur has a bad habit of flirting with women in a sort of overbearing way that not everyone appreciates. So what if he took things too far and one of his victims decided to take a stand? And we know that Garret Root tried to kiss his colleague at that Christmas party—he admitted it himself. So what if that wasn't the only thing he's guilty of? And Clint Bearman admitted to pulling his cat's tail as a kid, so we all know what that man is capable of. Is it too crazy to assume he would join an association of pet torturers?" She took a deep breath. "And you have to admit that Douglas looks like a heartbreaker, so maybe he broke one heart too many and she decided not to stand for his nonsense."

"But what about Chase?" asked Brutus, ready to defend his human. "Surely you don't believe for one moment that he's guilty of anything like that?"

"No, I don't," said Harriet defensively. "But he is a cop, and he has arrested a lot of people over the course of his career. So it's not inconceivable that someone decided to file a complaint against him and get some of his own back. That doesn't mean the complaint has merit, but Uncle Alec is obligated to investigate any complaint."

She was right, of course. It was entirely possible that some or even all of these rumors that were circulating about these people—most of them men, I had noticed—had a kernel of truth. And the fact that they were all converging at the same moment in time was simply a coincidence. And if that were the case, there was no case. Or there were a lot of cases against men who thought they could act with impunity when they should have known better.

"But what about Kingman?" asked Dooley. "Surely he's innocent, right?"

Harriet smiled. "I don't think any of us is assuming that the allegations leveled against Kingman are connected with the other cases, Dooley. But it is true that Kingman likes the ladies a little too much, so maybe one of them was fed up."

We had arrived at the General Store, more out of habit than anything else, but of course the shop was closed, and of Kingman there was no trace, since he had gone home with Wilbur—our home, not his own—just to be on the safe side.

For a moment, we glanced up at the storefront, and I think we all felt a little bereaved that the central meeting place of all cats of Hampton Cove would have been closed down for business. The window had been spray-painted with slogans that aren't fit to print, and the door had been boarded up, presumably after it had been smashed in and the place vandalized.

As we sat there, Buster crossed the street and approached us.

"Oh, hey, Buster," I said. "So how was cat choir last night?"

He gave me a sad look. "After you left, things got a little out of hand. Musti and Kitty picked a fight with some of the older cats, and they up and left."

"What did they fight about?" asked Harriet.

"I think things turned sour when Kitty demanded we swear a sort of oath of allegiance to her and Musti. She said

145

they felt that some of us were still in league with Shanille and were plotting to get rid of them. So we had to promise that we wouldn't talk to Shanille ever again, and they even made us come up with all the bad things we could think of. They called it a purification. A cleansing. A way to get rid of the past and herald in a new era for our local cat community. So when some of the older cats felt uncomfortable with that, Kitty told them to get lost."

"So it's either Shanille or Musti and Kitty?" I asked. "Two camps?"

"Something like that," Buster admitted ruefully. "Though I've got to be honest with you guys. I don't feel comfortable with that either. I like Shanille, and I don't see why we have to say all these bad things about her and shun her from now on."

"Are you even supposed to talk to us, Buster?" asked Brutus. "Seeing as we're all friends with Shanille? My enemy's friends are my enemies, right?"

Buster gave him a startled look. "But I *want* to be friends with you guys. I want to be friends with *everyone*. Why all this division and this strife?"

"It's a power game," said Harriet. "Kitty and Musti are trying to take over control of Hampton Cove's cat community. They've identified Shanille as one of its leaders, and now they're trying to destroy her and take her place. No idea why, since Shanille isn't much of a leader at all. In fact, we don't have any leaders."

"Harriet is right," I said. "We're cats. We don't follow leaders."

But clearly, Kitty and Musti didn't see it that way.

"They said some very mean things about you, by the way, Max," said Buster.

"Me!" I said.

"Yeah, they said you fancy yourself some kind of detective

when you're just a fat cat with an ego to match the size of your gut." He winced as I stared at him. "Their words, not mine!"

"This is too much," I said, much annoyed. "I'll have you know that my gut isn't that big." I pointed to the body part. "It's pure muscle—hard as a rock!"

Brutus now gave my belly a poke. It made a sort of ploinking sound. "Hard as a marshmallow, you mean," he said with a grin.

"Very funny, Brutus," I said.

"They said some bad things about you, too, Brutus," said Buster, who was on a roll now. "They said you're simply a nasty bully—and ugly, too."

Brutus's eyes went wide. "I'm not ugly! I'll have you know that in New York they called me Brutus the Magnificent, on account of the fact I'm so handsome!"

"What did they say about me?" asked Harriet curiously.

"That you're probably the vainest cat that has ever lived. And you can't sing."

Harriet's mouth opened and closed a few times, like a fish on dry land, before she managed to spit out, "I'll get them for this! Those nasty—"

"What did they say about me?" asked Dooley.

Buster blinked. "Nothing."

"Nothing?"

Buster shrugged. "Nothing at all. I guess they thought you weren't important enough to mention."

Dooley seemed inordinately happy about this. "Oh, that's good, isn't it? Looks like I'm the only one who isn't being canceled."

"I'm not being canceled," I said. "They just called me fat and stupid."

"And they called me nasty and ugly," Brutus growled unhappily.

"And they said I can't sing!" Harriet cried. "It's not fair!"

"Didn't anyone disagree with them?" I asked.

Buster gave me a sheepish look. "Apart from those older cats? No one."

"You didn't stand up for us, Buster?" asked Harriet.

Shamefacedly, Buster had to admit that he hadn't. "I guess I was afraid to be called out myself. Or shunned from the group. The atmosphere wasn't pleasant."

No, I could see that it wasn't. Cat choir had definitely turned into something it was never meant to be. And if Kitty and Musti were left unchecked, they'd soon poison the atmosphere in our entire town, making things unpleasant for everyone.

But before we could discuss how to resolve this matter and put those two in their place, Garret Root's beagle Susan came trotting up to us. He looked distressed. "Oh, I finally found you guys," he said. "You have to come quick. It's Garret. I can't seem to wake him up!"

CHAPTER 30

*M*erle Hartfield took a sip from his coffee as he flipped the pages of his newspaper. At his feet, his faithful bulldog Cyrus lay, gazing up at him from time to time with expectant eyes. Cyrus knew that by the time Merle had finished his coffee and had flipped the final page of his paper, the time had come to take him out for his morning walk. It was a time-honored tradition they had established when Merle and his wife Deirdre had first brought Cyrus home from the pound, and it amused Deirdre that Cyrus would keep her husband to it.

"Nothing in the paper again," he grumbled as he skipped the comics and turned straight to the sports section. "Sometimes I wonder why we still get it."

"Drink your coffee and take Cyrus for his walk," his wife instructed as she finished replanting her African violets in a bigger pot. She stood back and admired her handiwork with satisfaction. "There. That should do the trick," she murmured. Whereas he was more the man of handling anything to do with the house, Deirdre's main passion was her backyard, and more specifically, the wealth of plants and flowers that flourished there and had earned her the admiration of the entire neighborhood.

Merle quickly glanced at the personal ads, and was about to put the paper down when a short headline caught his attention. 'Beef with someone?' the headline read. 'Call this number for a permanent solution that won't break the bank.'

"Huh," he said as he read the short and unassuming ad again. Now what could that be about? As it happened, he did have a beef with someone. A pretty big beef, in fact. Twice already he'd been passed over for a promotion he felt was rightfully his. And twice a younger colleague had been promoted instead of him. The person he blamed for this gross injustice was his boss Ryan Tuthill, who, for some reason he didn't understand, seemed to carry a grudge against him. As a loyal employee of the DMV, by rights he should have been promoted to a higher position a long time ago. The fact that he was stuck at a lower position stung, and stung something bad.

He glanced up at his wife but knew better than to broach the subject, which frankly they'd already beaten to death these last couple of years. If he even mentioned his boss or his promotion again, she simply rolled her eyes and told him to move on. In her opinion, it didn't matter if he was promoted or not, since they earned enough to afford a comfortable lifestyle. And in a sense, she was right. But it still hurt to see those younger colleagues having passed him by on the train of life. To the extent that he couldn't move on. And he couldn't let it go.

He folded the paper, drained his mug, and got up.

Cyrus's ears pricked up, and he emitted a surprised but hopeful whimper, as if he couldn't believe it was finally happening.

"Come, boy," said Merle and headed into the hallway, where Cyrus's leash hung next to the coat rack.

More whimpering, this time at a higher pitch. The moment Merle grabbed the leash, Cyrus started jumping up against his leg, then gamboling up and down the hallway until Merle managed to put the leash on him and open the front door.

"I'm taking Cyrus for a walk," he hollered.

"Don't forget to buy milk," she yelled back.

As he left the house and pulled the door shut, he took his phone out of his pocket. He had memorized the number from the mysterious ad, and after a pause, he punched it in and put the phone to his ear.

"Permanent Solutions, Inc," a pleasant male voice said on the other end.

"Ah, I saw your ad in the paper this morning," he said. "So I was wondering if you could tell me some more about these permanent solutions you mentioned?"

"By all means," said the pleasant voice. "Do you have a beef with someone?"

"I do, yeah. With my boss. He keeps passing me over for promotion."

"At Permanent Solutions, we deal with people like your boss all the time."

"You're not… into anything illegal, are you?" he asked, figuring the term 'permanent solution' sounded a little ominous, as if they'd hire a hitman to get rid of the guy.

"Nothing illegal whatsoever," said the voice. "Why don't we arrange to meet? Then you can tell me all about that boss of yours, and I will tell you how to make sure that he never passes you up for promotion ever again. How does that sound?"

"Too good to be true!" he said with a laugh.

"I can assure you it's very true," said the man.

"How much would this set me back?" he asked.

"We have different packages," said the man. "Depending

on how permanent of a solution you're looking for, we have a Silver, Gold, and Platinum package. Silver will put your boss out of commission for a while, Gold will make sure he never holds you back again, and Platinum will permanently remove your boss from the equation—never to be heard from again."

When the guy gave him the numbers, he felt reasonably relaxed that he could afford the Silver package. And since his curiosity was seriously piqued, he decided to go for it. "Let's meet. And put me down for the Silver package."

Deirdre didn't even have to know about it.

And it was probably best if she didn't.

* * *

TRESSA WAS FEELING A LITTLE BLUE. After her disastrous date with Douglas last night, sleep had eluded her for most of the night, and by the time she finally dozed off, her alarm had sounded, announcing a new day. She had been looking forward to hashing the whole thing out with her friend and colleague Bonnie, but much to her surprise, Bonnie's desk remained empty, and when she sent her a text to ask where she was, Bonnie messaged back to say she was going to a job interview and not to mention anything to their supervisor.

'A new job?' she asked.

'Yeah. Something really exciting. Will tell you more later.'

'Good luck!'

On the one hand, she was glad for her friend, of course. Bonnie had been talking about leaving the syndicate for a while and finding a job with higher pay and better benefits. On the other hand, she would miss her buddy. Now who would she complain to about the blows that life occasionally dealt her? And who was she going to share a coffee with so they could gossip about their other colleagues?

Though when she passed the Happy Bean that morning, she had noticed a sign that said it was closed due to personal circumstances, so it looked as if their favorite place to hang out was out of commission for the time being. She had already decided she would never go back there anyway. Not after the way Douglas had treated her, and then lied to her about his sister being pregnant.

And as she sat staring before her for a moment, she suddenly grabbed her phone again and texted, 'Ask them if they can use a second person, will you?'

This time no response came, which told her all she needed to know.

Looked like she was on her own from now on.

CHAPTER 31

*W*e arrived at our destination in due course, with Susan leading the way. The house where Garret was staying belonged to his brother, as he had already indicated that morning during the meeting of the Canceled Anonymous.

"He was fine when he left Odelia's office," said Brutus as Susan led us around the back of the house, which was a nice villa in a quiet and leafy neighborhood. "He must have taken a turn for the worse the moment he got home."

"Maybe he realized how hopeless his situation is," said Harriet. "That's why it's so important to establish a buddy system. So members of the CA can call a buddy when they're feeling low. Chase could be Garret's buddy, or one of the other members."

"I should have gone with him," said Susan. "But I was busy sniffing out a pile of bones in the backyard, and by the time I realized they were chicken bones, Garret had already left. Then when he came back he seemed fine. Happy, even."

"It's often that way," said Harriet. "They put on a brave

face for the outside world, but once they're alone, they collapse."

"His brother isn't home?" I asked.

"I'm not sure," said Susan. "I looked for him everywhere, but when I couldn't find him, I decided to try and find you guys."

The house hadn't been outfitted with a pet door, which was an inconvenience, but one of the downstairs windows had been left open, and so we snuck in that way. "Jim has been promising Garret he will install a pet door," Susan explained as we hopped down from the windowsill. "But he hasn't gotten around to it yet."

"So Garret is planning to stay here for the time being?" I asked.

"I think so. Or at least as long as this campaign is going on."

He took us through the kitchen and into the corridor, then up the stairs. When we arrived on the landing, we heard voices coming from one of the front rooms, and Susan stiffened. "That's odd," he said. "I could have sworn he was out."

"Is that Garret's brother?" I asked.

"Yeah, that's Jim's voice. And it's coming from his office."

He then led us to one of the bedrooms, and as he pushed open the door with his nose, we saw a man lying on the bed, and he wasn't moving.

"Oh, no," said Harriet. "Looks like we're too late!"

To ascertain whether she was right, we all hopped onto the bed. And as Susan gave his human a slight shove with his paw, the man uttered a sound, causing us to breathe out a sigh of relief.

"He's alive," said Susan. "But he's not moving!"

"Maybe shove him harder," Brutus suggested.

Susan did as he was told and gave his human a hard shove. This time the sound Garret produced was more one of annoyance, like a human who's fast asleep and doesn't want to wake up.

I glanced over to the nightstand, and much to my satisfaction, I didn't see any pill boxes or anything of that nature. I did see a large bottle of alcohol that was half empty, so that might explain why the man couldn't be awakened.

"Here, let me try," said Brutus, who hates prevarication. And so he unsheathed a series of very sharp-looking claws and proceeded to dig them into the man's arm!

"Hey, what do you think you're doing!" said Susan.

"Acupuncture," said Brutus with a grin. "Works every time."

He was right, for Garret's eyes suddenly sprang open, and then he let out a blood-curdling scream and sat up with a jerk.

"See?" said our friend. "Sure-fire method."

"But he's bleeding," said Susan.

"You can't make an omelet without breaking a couple of eggs."

We watched closely as Garret glanced around, blinking in confusion. Then he looked down at his arm, where a nice series of puncture marks had appeared and said, "Ouch!"

"So how are things, Garret?" asked Brutus, after assuming the role of acupuncturist, now also fashioning himself to be something of a psychotherapist.

But of course Garret couldn't understand what he was saying. Instead, he gave Brutus a very unfriendly look. "You did this!" he said accusingly.

"With the best intentions," Brutus said. "It woke you up, didn't it?"

"What... what are these cats doing here?" asked Garret. "How did they get in?" Then he fastened his eyes on me and frowned. "Aren't you Odelia Kingsley's cat?"

"Yep, that's me," I confirmed, oddly pleased that he would have recognized me.

At the meeting that morning, there had been some confusion when Garret claimed that the Odelia Kingsley he knew was an elderly lady, and not the young woman he met at her office. But then when Gran walked in, the confusion had been cleared up when she explained she hadn't wanted to dissuade him from the notion that she was Odelia because of the precarious mental state she had found him in. "Better two Odelias than no Odelia at all," she argued. The matter had soon been settled, and Garret accepted her apologies for the misrepresentation.

The man now pressed his hands to his face and suddenly burst into tears!

"Um…" said Brutus with a frown. "Okay, so it wasn't my intention to hurt you, bud."

"I don't think he's crying from the physical pain," I said. Clearly, the man was going through some kind of emotional turmoil.

"They're cutting me from the will," he lamented.

We shared a look of surprise.

"What will?" I asked.

"Can you believe it?" said Garret. "Just because I'm being accused of something I didn't do, they're cutting me from the will. My own parents!"

"Oh, poor guy," said Harriet. She turned to Susan. "Did you know about this?"

"Well, I knew that his parents were thinking about selling their house and dividing the money between their three kids, but no, I didn't know they were cutting him from the will."

The man was seriously weeping now, and I think we all felt a little uncomfortable having to witness this personal tragedy. I mean, it's one thing to save a man from himself, but another to assume the role of personal confessor.

And so we decided to remove ourselves from the scene for the time being and give the guy some privacy. After all, we had done our bit and had ascertained that the man was alive and well—or at least more or less so.

Walking out of the room, we convened in the corridor.

"I think Garret should talk to someone," I said.

"He needs a buddy," Harriet reiterated.

"Yeah, I guess you're right," I said.

And so we decided to go and get Odelia to assign Garret a buddy he could tell his problems to and unburden his troubled heart.

"Why are they cutting him from their will?" asked Dooley.

"Because they're disappointed in him?" Harriet suggested.

"They had a family dinner last night," said Susan. "So they must have told him about their decision then." He shook his head sadly. "Looks like they've decided that the rumors about their son are true after all. Poor guy."

"Yeah, poor guy," said Brutus, who was licking his paws.

The door to Garret's brother's office opened, and a woman appeared. She shook the man's hand and thanked him profusely for the opportunity he had offered.

"What's that all about?" I asked.

"Jim runs his business from his home," Susan explained.

"What business is he in?"

"Oh, I don't know. Some online consultancy thing. Sounds boring."

I nodded as I studied the woman saying goodbye and leaving via the stairs. Jim closed the door to his office, and for a moment, all was quiet. Then downstairs, a door slammed as the woman left the house, and voices sounded when Jim took a call. Somehow, and don't ask me why, I felt compelled to listen in on that call.

And so I quietly crept up to the door and put my ear against the panel.

It wasn't long before I got the impression that Jim's job was anything but boring. Some might even call it illegal. It certainly explained a lot of what had been going on in Hampton Cove of late. And as I sat there listening with rising indignation, suddenly the door opened, and I found myself face to face with Jim.

For a moment, I was afraid he would grab me and personally cancel me!

"It's just a stupid cat," he spoke into the phone. Then he caught sight of my friends. "God, how did they get in? Must be my dumbass brother again. First that dog of his, and now these cats." He pressed the phone to his chest and bellowed, "Garret! Get rid of these cats, will you? Before they poop all over my rug!"

We all stared up at the man with extreme distress.

And as I thrust out my chest, I said, "I will have you know, sir, that we're not in the habit of pooping all over anything. We're clean and proper cats."

"That's right," said Brutus. "We're perfectly capable of distinguishing between a rug and our litter box."

"The man is crazy," was Harriet's opinion. "And frankly I take umbrage."

"Why does he want us to poop on his rug, Max?" asked Dooley.

But before I could respond, Jim yelled again, "Garret!"

"I'm coming," said Garret, hurrying out of his room.

"The cats?" said Jim, giving his brother a warning look. Then he placed the phone to his ear again. "I'm sorry about that. Where were we?" And he disappeared into his office again, carefully closing the door as he did.

Garret shook his head and tsk-tsked a little. "Now what am I going to do with you?" he said. He crouched down until his eyes were level with mine. "You look like a clever kitty. So what are you doing here, huh? Did Odelia send you? Is this her way of making sure I'm all right? Cause I can assure you that I'm fine. I mean, I may not look fine, but that meeting this morning did me a world of good."

It was then that I got an idea, and so I pointed to the door of his brother's office. He gave me a curious look. "Why do I get the impression you're trying to tell me something?"

"Cause I am!" I said.

Amused, he approached the door of the office and placed his ear against it, assuming I was trying to play a game. It didn't take long before that look of amusement fell from his face, to be replaced by a look of horror.

"Oh, dear Lord," he murmured. Then stared at me with new appreciation. He gave me a nod, which I returned in kind. Then he tiptoed away from the door again and hurried into his room to fetch his phone.

Moments later, he was in communication with Odelia, telling her about what we had both discovered. I think it's safe to say that by now he wasn't too well pleased with his brother.

"What's going on, Max?" asked Harriet.

"Jim Root has been a very naughty boy," I said.

CHAPTER 32

The problem was that Chase had been suspended, so he couldn't do the honors. And Odelia wasn't a civilian consultant anymore, so she couldn't get involved either. Gran and Scarlett would have been happy to place Jim under arrest, but Uncle Alec didn't like it when they overstepped the boundaries of their brief, and so the only person available was Chase's colleague Wade Westen.

The man arrived in his squad car—which I'll remind you had been Chase's squad car until his suspension—and carried himself with a certain modicum of swagger, clearly very happy with himself and his new position. Chase and Odelia were there, to lend support, and also Uncle Alec himself, to make sure that his underling did everything by the book. Gran and Scarlett had turned up, as representatives of the neighborhood watch, and last but not least Garret and Jim's sister, since she was in the neighborhood, and was surprised by the hullabaloo.

In due course, Jim was placed under arrest, and even though he protested his innocence in a very vocal manner, the moment his phone was confiscated, preparatory to putting it in evidence, he quickly piped down. More officers arrived, and carried out a search of the house, focusing on Jim's office, and when finally Jim was being led out through the front door, Garret gave him a look of accusation. "You did this," he said, pointing a finger at his younger brother.

"He did what?" asked their sister. "Garret, what's going on?"

"He set up this whole thing!" said Garret.

"What thing? What are you talking about?"

"The, the thing—the gossip. The rumors."

Cristy blinked, clearly having a hard time following her brother's rambling style of conversation. "I'm afraid you're not making a lot of sense, Garret."

"Tell her," said Garret. "Go on, tell her!"

Jim rolled his eyes. "Oh, fine. So I launched a couple of rumors. Big deal."

"You destroyed my life!"

"Don't be so melodramatic, Garret."

"You got me fired from my job!"

"You hate your job!"

"He's right, Garret," said Cristy. "You've been complaining about your job for years."

"Tell her about Clint," said Garret, folding his arms across his chest.

Cristy looked up as if stung. "Clint? What about Clint?"

"He wasn't the right guy for you, sis," said Jim. "I did you a favor."

Cristy blinked. "You… it was you? But I thought…"

"Clint isn't a pet torturer, Cris," said Garret. "The guy wouldn't hurt a fly."

Cristy's face had turned a bright red, and she was balling her fists now. "You launched that rumor about the pet torture? You made me call off my engagement?"

"He was wrong for you! All wrong!"

"Oh, you horrible little…" And before anyone could stop her, she was accosting her own brother, hammering him with her tiny fists, until he broke into a run. And as they disappeared out of sight, Officer Wade gave his boss an uncertain look.

"Well, go after them, you idiot!" said Uncle Alec. "Before he escapes!"

"Yes, boss," said the officer, and hurried after the brother and sister.

We saw the three of them come around the house a second time, then a third time, with Officer Wade looking more and more fatigued each time, so the fourth time, Chase felt that enough was enough and grabbed Jim by the collar.

"I can't believe you would do that to me!" said Cristy, who was out of breath, but not as much as the officer who had been chasing her and her brother.

"He did a lot more than that," said Garret darkly. "I overheard him discussing his new business venture with his business partner this morning, and he's made dozens of victims."

"I wouldn't exactly call them victims," said Jim, panting a little. "I'm sure all of them did something to deserve what happened to them."

"What did I do to deserve being suspended?" asked Chase, who had attached himself to Jim's collar and clearly wasn't about to let go.

"Oh, I don't know," said Jim evasively. "You're a cop. So I'm sure you annoyed plenty of people over the course of a long career. Sooner or later karma will catch up with you."

Uncle Alec shook his head. "You got me to suspend my best detective, all for some unsubstantiated rumors?"

"Who was the client?" Chase now demanded.

Jim looked away.

"Answer him!" Uncle Alec said.

Jim cut a quick glance to Officer Wade, who stood with

his hands on his knees recovering from the exertion. When he felt everyone's eyes on him, he looked up. "What?" he asked.

"Did you do this?" asked Chase. "Did you get me suspended so you could steal my job?"

"Absolutely not!" said the officer, but he didn't sound very convincing.

"It was his dad," said Jim. "He paid me to get his son the promotion he felt he deserved. And since there's only one detective position on the team, my job was to get rid of you so the client's son could step into the job. It worked like a charm."

"My God," said Uncle Alec, making a gesture of disgust.

"Hey, don't shoot the messenger," said Jim. "I only did what people asked me to do."

"How did it work, exactly?" asked Odelia.

"Oh, you know. You launch a rumor online, post it on the different social media sites, and before you know it, people will run with it and start sharing, and it spreads. You'd be surprised how people love to gossip and spread bad news."

"And the petitions?" asked Gran. "That was you?"

"Of course that was me," said Jim, who seemed to take particular pride in his job. "All of it was me. And I've got customers lining up to give me more business. In fact, this is the most successful business venture I've ever been involved in."

"Who is your business partner?" asked Odelia.

Jim jerked his thumb at Officer Wade. "His dad. He's a successful businessman in his own right, so he recognized a good thing when he saw it. After I secured his son the position, he decided to invest heavily in my company. Allow me to expand."

"I didn't know about that," said Wade, holding up his hands. "Any of it."

"That remains to be seen," said Uncle Alec sternly. "As of right now, you're suspended, Wade. And you," he told Chase, "are reinstated. Effective immediately."

"What about me?" asked Odelia.

Uncle Alec smiled. "You can consider yourself part of the team again."

"And what about me?" asked Gran. "Am I also part of the team?"

Uncle Alec's smile faded. "Let's not go there, shall we?"

It was Chase who got to do the honors of escorting Jim Root to the squad car, which apparently was his again, and took off in a cloud of smoke.

"But... how am I supposed to get home now?" asked Wade.

"You walk," said Uncle Alec curtly, and took off in the direction of his own car.

As we stood waiting on the sidewalk for Odelia to bring her car around, suddenly the same woman who I'd seen walking out of Jim's office parked her car and got out. When she saw the small gathering, she hesitated, but then approached regardless. "What's going on?" she asked.

"Who are you?" asked Gran.

"Bonnie Gallacher. I work for Jim Root?"

Gran's eyes narrowed. "So you're part of the gang, are you? Odelia!" she bellowed. "Here's another one!"

"Another what?" asked the woman.

Odelia, who had come hurrying up, regarded her closely. "You work for Jim Root?"

"I do," the woman confirmed. "I was hired by him this morning. He forgot to sign my contract, though. I just noticed so I figured I'd get it signed. I want to give my notice at my current job, so I wanted to make sure everything was legal."

"Oh, things are far from legal," Gran assured her.

"You've been hoodwinked," Scarlett said.

"Hoodwinked? What do you mean?"

"Jim Root was just arrested," Odelia explained.

"Arrested! But why?"

"He's been operating an online scam," said Gran.

"Well, not a scam," Scarlett specified. "He's been setting up gossip campaigns that get people into trouble with their bosses and their friends and neighbors."

Bonnie swallowed away a lump. "Oh, but that's horrible."

"What did he say he wanted to hire you for?" asked Odelia.

"Admin, mainly," said Bonnie. "I was to work as his PA."

"He didn't specify his business?"

"He said he was into online marketing?"

Gran produced a scoffing sound. "Some marketing."

"You have to admit he was successful at what he did," said Scarlett. "Even though it was extremely illegal and morally reprehensible."

"Okay, so I guess I'm out of a new job then," said Bonnie. "Good thing I didn't hand in my notice at my current job." And so she took off, and soon we all did. And it was as we were riding back to town with Odelia that I started to wonder how we could possibly repair all of the damage that Jim had done.

CHAPTER 33

Tressa was surprised to see her friend and colleague suddenly turn up that afternoon. The moment their supervisor's back was turned, she whispered, "So how did the job interview go?"

Bonnie rolled her eyes. "The guy was arrested by the police literally within an hour of the interview. So I was hired, but now he's in jail, so I guess the job isn't available anymore."

She refused to say more, and since Tressa didn't want to get her friend in trouble by revealing that she was looking to leave the syndicate, she kept her tongue. They could discuss the whole thing later on when they were out of the office. At which point she wanted to ask Bonnie's advice about Douglas. The guy had sent her a text apologizing for last night and said he had a good reason to do what he did. She wondered if she should hear him out or confront him with the horrible rumors that were circulating about him online. She had to admit that she felt tempted to meet up and give him the opportunity to offer his side of the story. But before she did, she wanted to ask Bonnie.

It was later that afternoon that a news item appeared online about a man being arrested that morning in connection to a case of online harassment. She wondered if this could be the man Bonnie was referring to. But when she asked her about it, she seemed reluctant to comment.

"It's all ancient history anyway," said Bonnie. "I gambled, and I lost."

It caused Tressa to wonder what she meant by that. Her friend seemed strangely withdrawn and couldn't be induced to discuss the case with her, even as it started to attract a lot of attention and soon became the most-discussed news item amongst their colleagues.

"Do NOT tell them that I applied for a job with that guy!" Bonnie warned her at some point when even their supervisor commented on the strange case.

"Of course not," said Tressa. "Who do you take me for?"

She felt a little hurt that Bonnie would think she would ever betray her confidence. So when her friend had to slip out to go to the bathroom, she decided to put a little note on her desk, assuring her once more that her secret was safe with her. She rummaged through Bonnie's drawer in search of a piece of paper, and as she did, she suddenly saw Douglas's face appear. Her hand stayed for a moment, but as she picked up the photograph, she saw that it showed both Douglas and Bonnie and was one of those snapshots you take at a photo booth. She stared at it for a moment, not fully understanding what she was seeing. As she revealed more of the strip of pictures, she saw that the last one in the lineup showed Douglas and Bonnie... kissing!

"But..." she murmured.

Bonnie had never mentioned that she and Douglas used to date. How odd was that? Now why wouldn't she mention that?

She checked the back of the picture and saw that Bonnie

had scribbled a date on it. Four years ago. Long before Tressa had ever expressed an interest in Douglas. Long before she had even laid eyes on the man.

Just then, she sensed a presence next to her, and as she looked up, she saw that Bonnie stood looking at her with blazing eyes. "Give me that!" she snapped and snatched the pictures from Tressa's hand.

"You and Douglas used to be an item?" she asked.

Reluctantly, Bonnie nodded. "We went out on one date."

"But why didn't you tell me?"

"What's there to tell? We went out once, and he wasn't interested in repeating the experience, so I must have made a pretty terrible impression on him." She sounded bitter about it, even four years on. "He didn't even recognize me when he opened his coffee shop, and I was one of his first customers. Great date, huh?"

"I'm so sorry, Bonnie," she said. "If I had known, I would never have…"

Bonnie turned on her. "You wouldn't have what, Tressa? Fallen for the guy?"

"Well, no. I mean, I would never have gone out with him."

"Oh, don't give me that," said Bonnie viciously. "Of course you would have gone out with him. And why not? It was just the one date, big deal."

"Obviously, it was a big deal to you," she said.

And much to her surprise, suddenly Bonnie burst into tears. She plunked down on her chair and buried her face in her hands as she wailed up a storm. But when Candace came hurrying over, Tressa held up her hand. Clearly, the last thing Bonnie needed was for their supervisor to stick her nose in.

She placed an arm around her friend's quaking shoulders. Finally, the weeping subsided, and Bonnie turned a teary red face up to her. "I did something really terrible, Tressa," she confessed.

"What did you do?"

But Bonnie wouldn't say.

Instead, she grabbed her bag and practically ran from the office.

Whatever it was, it must have been something bad, she thought.

Then, on a hunch, she decided to dig through her friend's drawer some more. Which is when she discovered more snapshots with other men.

The first one was called Clint Bearman, according to the name scribbled on the back. And the second was Garret Root. Oddly enough, those names had also popped up in the news story that had been developing all day, as the victims of Jim Root, the man who had devised a way to weaponize and monetize online gossip campaigns.

And as Tressa sat back, she wondered for the first time if she should tell the police about this.

CHAPTER 34

For the last couple of days, both Odelia and Chase had been very busy. Odelia by writing a series of articles denouncing the campaigns Jim Root had set up, and restoring the reputations of the people he had targeted. And Chase by interviewing Jim and getting to the bottom of his system and the people involved. As it turned out, his very first client was a woman who felt wronged by the men she had dated and had asked him to help her get revenge on them. As a skilled online marketer, he had seen it as a challenge, and when he was successful in getting the woman the revenge she was looking for, he had decided to expand his business. Eventually, she had applied for a job, and no doubt they would have made the perfect team.

"So Garret Root used to date this Bonnie person?" asked Harriet.

"That's right," I said. "They went out on two dates, and then Garret felt they weren't compatible, and the third date never materialized."

"But Bonnie felt wronged."

"Because she kept being stood up," I explained. "And in

the end, it made her resent these men and decide to get back at them for not treating her with the respect she felt she deserved. So she got Garret fired from his job, Clint Bearman fired from his job and his engagement terminated, and Douglas forced to close down his coffee shop."

"That wasn't a very nice thing to do," said Dooley.

"No, it certainly wasn't," I agreed.

The four of us were seated on the porch swing in Marge and Tex's backyard, with the humans gathered around the garden table in preparation for a family meal being cooked up by the good doctor, whose career was finally on track again after the complaint made against him turned out to be bogus.

Marge had been allowed to return to the library when she had been identified as one of Jim Root's many victims. And Wilbur Vickery had been able to reopen his shop when his name had also featured on Jim's long list of targets.

"I can't understand why anyone would target Marge," said Harriet.

"A competing librarian wanting to take a shortcut," said Brutus.

As with Chase, a young and ambitious person had decided that she didn't want to wait until opportunity knocked but had wanted to get rid of the competition by removing Marge from the equation. Whereas in Wilbur's case, it had been a real estate developer eager to get his hands on Wilbur's shop so he could turn it into condos.

"Who was the client in Tex's case?" asked Brutus.

"Another doctor from a different town, actually," I said. "Who wanted to take over Tex's practice on the cheap." And it would have worked if Jim hadn't been caught. The man was running so many smear campaigns that sooner or later he would have been found out, with people being canceled by the dozens.

"So what about Melody Jarram?" asked Harriet.

"What about her?"

"Well, she did file a complaint against Garret."

"She retracted her complaint when she discovered the truth about the campaign against him. Turns out she mainly faulted him for not following up on that kiss they shared at the Christmas party last year. They're dating now."

"They are?" said Harriet, surprised.

"Well, they've arranged for a first date. Taking things slow and easy."

"But I thought Garret didn't even like her? Didn't he complain to their principal?"

"I guess their relationship is complicated." As is often the case with humans.

"What I don't understand is why Jim would target his own brother and sister," said Brutus. "That seems extremely callous of the man."

"Not at all," I said. "It shows his business sense. By discrediting Garret and Cristy, because of the bad match she made, causing her parents to lose a lot of money on the canceled wedding, he managed to convince them that he was the only one of the three siblings who was making a success of himself. And so he had persuaded them to make him a substantial gift and cut his brother and sister out of their will. The man is nothing if not a ruthless and clever operator."

Now that he was in prison, hopefully his mom and dad would realize they had been bamboozled, just like a lot of people in Hampton Cove had been taken for a ride, and restore Garret and Cristy's birthright.

"So what about that spiked cookie business?" asked Harriet.

"Turns out that Natalie Francis was behind that after all," I said.

Now that Wade Westen was no longer running the show, Chase had looked a little more closely at Mrs. Francis, and it wasn't long before he discovered that Mr. Francis had set up a lucrative side business as a cannabis grower and pot dealer, enlisting his wife for logistical support. Unfortunately Mrs. Francis, while whipping up a batch of cookies for the school fundraiser, had accidentally added an ingredient she shouldn't have in the form of her husband's prime weed.

"At least no one suffered any permanent damage," said Brutus.

"Yeah, at least there's that," I agreed.

Chase, who was assisting his father-in-law in whipping up some tasty morsels on the grill, looked happy and relaxed now that he had his job back. The only one who wasn't celebrating was Uncle Alec, who felt that he'd wronged his deputy to some extent. But as the others had told him, he couldn't possibly have known.

All in all things had ended well for all involved, except maybe for us cats, who were still at loggerheads with a pair of usurpers, as Shanille had called Musti and Kitty. And so after we'd had our fill of food, we announced to Odelia that we were taking our leave. We had urgent business in the park, where a special meeting of dog choir had been arranged—or 'the choir of the canceled,' as it had been named.

Before long, we were on our way to the park. Darkness was slowly setting in, and by the time we arrived at our destination and joined the rest of our friends, a certain hardening of our moods took place. "If Kitty and Musti so much as talk to me," Harriet warned. "I'll give them a piece of my mind they'll never forget."

"They won't show their faces here," said Brutus. "Not if they know what's good for them."

Garret's beagle Susan had also joined dog choir, and so if

174

Kitty and Musti and their acolytes dared to approach, they would encounter some stiff resistance. But since the main reason we enjoyed gathering in the park was to develop our musical talents, we decided not to dwell on the demise of cat choir and to celebrate the choir that had adopted us by giving of our best.

And so Shanille took up her position as conductor, a motley collection of cats and dogs assembled in their assigned locations, and before long, we were all singing our hearts out and were actually having a great time. Oddly enough, as we sang, more and more cats walked up to join us, and I recognized many of them as former members of cat choir. Others stood to the side and listened, and more than one of them actually had tears in their eyes, especially when Harriet regaled us with one of her fabled solos, proving she was in excellent form.

The meeting turned sour when all of a sudden Kitty and Musti themselves showed up. Much to my surprise, they appeared to be isolated from the rest of their following, turning up without their usual posse of fawning devotees.

Instead of halting the proceedings, we kept on singing, in a sense daring them to shut us down and declare dog choir extinct, just as they'd done with cat choir.

When the final note died away, for a moment no one spoke, then loud cheers rang out, with all of those looking on clearly moved by the performance we'd delivered. It certainly filled me with a sense of pride, and Harriet even took a bow as shouts for an encore filled the air.

But then Kitty and Musti stepped to the fore, and the cheers died away.

"That was beautiful," said Musti, and I fully expected her to follow that up with some kind of caustic remark, of the kind I'd gotten used to from the twosome. But instead, she wiped away a tear. "I don't know if you've heard, but Kitty and I are moving away again. Our human has been arrested and is being accused of some terrible things, so her sister has graciously offered to take us in for now. She lives in Boston, so first thing tomorrow we'll be moving out there."

We all shared a look of surprise, but then I suddenly remembered that Kitty and Musti's human was called Bonnie. Apparently, this was the same Bonnie who had set Jim Root on his path of online destruction.

"We just wanted to tell you all that we feel that things got a little out of hand these last couple of days," Kitty said. "I guess we got carried away to some extent, and for that, we both want to offer our deepest apologies. If we insulted some of you, we're very sorry. And if we gave the impression that we are against singing as a form of creative expression, we apologize."

"Were you behind the campaign against Kingman?" a voice rang out.

Kitty and Musti shared a look, then both bowed their heads. "Yes, we were," said Musti.

"But why? What did Kingman ever do to you?"

Kitty sighed. "Nothing. Kingman never did anything to us. We just felt that if we were going to find our footing in Hampton Cove we needed to aim high and get rid of the cats in charge, and the first name anyone we asked mentioned was that of Kingman. Some even called him Hampton Cove's unofficial mayor. So we figured that once we got rid of him, we would be on velvet."

"And the second person cats mentioned was Shanille," said Musti. "So she had to go as well."

"But why get rid of us? Why this drive to be in charge?" asked Shanille.

Kitty gave her a rueful look. "I guess we're more ambitious than most?"

"Yeah, you're all happy to be followers," said Musti. "With

someone else leading the charge. But that's not us. We don't like to follow anyone. So we figured the only way forward was to become leaders of this community ourselves."

"You've got an odd way of being leaders," said Harriet.

"Yeah, a real leader doesn't try to get rid of the cats that are in charge," I said. "And besides, Kingman and Shanille aren't leaders because anyone put them in charge. They're leaders because of who they are, and how they conduct themselves and how they treat others. They're natural leaders, not chosen ones."

"Yeah, we see that now," said Kitty ruefully.

"Can we…" Musti suddenly looked nervous. "Can we join your choir, Shanille? It's just that… you all sounded so great just now. And you looked so joyful."

Shanille frowned. "You can join my choir, but only if you promise to behave."

"We promise," said Kitty and Musti in unison.

Much to our surprise, they both proved to be skilled singers, possessing angelic voices. And as we all launched into our next song, I think our neighbors expressed it best when they showered us with shoes, always a sign of great success.

I even got a brand-new Air Jordan aimed at my head, which I took in stride with a smile and which caused me to sing even louder than usual. Until Shanille sidled up to me and whispered, "Please stop singing, Max."

"Why?" I asked, much surprised.

"I don't know if you know this, but you can't carry a tune. You're distracting the others and causing them to sing off-key as well. So if you can simply mouth along and pretend to be singing, your conductor and the rest of the choir will be extremely grateful."

I closed my mouth with a click of the teeth.

"What's wrong, Max?" asked Dooley.

"Shanille says I sing out of tune."

"Oh, but we knew that already," he said, quite surprisingly.

"You knew that I can't sing?" I asked, staring at my friend.

"Of course. We all know that you can't sing. But we love you so much we don't say anything." He smiled. "I guess it's the volume that did you in this time. Usually you sing so quietly it doesn't bother anyone that you can't hit the right notes. But you were really belting, Max, and that's where the problem lies."

I opened and closed my mouth a couple of times. "But… but why hasn't anybody ever told me about this?"

"Like I said, we love you too much to upset you. But if you could just sing a little quieter, or even better: don't make any sound at all, that would be perfect."

Well, how about them apples?

Then Dooley raised his voice. "And now if Kingman could bring out his lute, I think we'd all enjoy an interlude. So let's give it up for Kingman and his lute!"

THE END

Thanks for reading! If you want to know when a new Nic Saint book comes out, sign up for Nic's mailing list: nicsaint.com/news

EXCERPT FROM PURRFECT VIRUS
(MAX 79)

Chapter One

Vesta had been jotting down a few random thoughts in her diary when she thought she heard a noise. She sat up a little straighter in bed—her favorite place to entrust her private musings to paper—and pricked up her ears. The sound seemed to come from the window, and as she slipped her feet from underneath the duvet—covered with drawings of orange cats as befits a self-confessed cat lady—she wondered if she shouldn't alert her son-in-law, no doubt still fast asleep in the room next to hers.

But then she decided against it. She prided herself on being a self-sufficient type of person who didn't need anything from anyone, and most definitely not from Tex, whom she had always considered something of an oaf. And so she tiptoed to the window, gripping her pen in her right hand as a weapon, hoping she wouldn't encounter a burglar or some other individual intent on perpetrating some nefarious designs on her person. If it was, she would give him or her the benefit of the sharp end of her pencil. After all, the pencil is still mightier than the sword.

When she arrived at the window, which was of the dormer variety, and looked out, she saw that the noise had originated from a large bird with black plumage, who seemed intent on hammering his way into the house by applying his sharp beak to the pane. If she wasn't mistaken, it was a raven—never a good sign!

She lowered the pencil and gave the bird a not-so-friendly look. "What do you want?" she asked in an irascible tone. If the bird understood what she was saying, it didn't give any indication, for it simply kept hammering away, as if its life depended on it. For a moment, she considered chasing it away, but then she had a better idea. Clearly, the bird was either laboring under a misapprehension that there was food to be had inside the house it was beleaguering with its presence, and it wasn't going to stop until it personally ascertained whether this was true or not, or it had some kind of urgent message to impart on its inhabitants.

So she tiptoed out of her room, barefoot across the wooden floor, and gently nudged open the door of her daughter and son-in-law's room. As she had surmised, two of their four cats were sound asleep at the foot of the bed. So she let out a noise like a steam whistle, causing all those resting in the bed to sit up with a jerk. She had intended to quietly whisper a word or two to the cats, but as usual, she didn't know the strength of her own voice.

The upshot was that both Tex and Marge were wide awake, and also Harriet and Brutus.

"There's a bird," she said in her defense. "I think it wants something. Could you..." She had addressed herself to Harriet and Brutus, but it was Marge who responded.

"Go back to bed, Ma," she said. And she immediately plunked down again to show her mother how it was done.

"Not... enough... sleep," Tex murmured as he followed his wife's example. He smacked his lips for a moment, giving his mother-in-law a sleepy look, and promptly dozed off again.

Lucky for Vesta, Harriet and Brutus were made of sterner stuff, and after she had given them a gesture that told them all they needed to know, they obediently hopped down from the bed and followed her into her own room.

"That's the bird," she said, gesturing to the black raven, still pecking away to its dark heart's content. "So if you could please ask what it wants?"

"I'm not sure this is such a good idea, Gran," said Harriet. "Birds, as a rule, startle easily."

"She's right," said Brutus. "The moment we jump up onto that windowsill, it will simply fly off."

They were absolutely right, of course. Birds and cats will probably never really see eye to eye, owing to differing viewpoints on the nature of food. Cats consider birds an essential staple of their diet, while birds take an entirely different view.

"Just ask what it wants," she said, "without going anywhere near it." When her cats continued to stare at her, she clarified, "Just holler, will you?"

Harriet smiled. She had finally understood. And so she cleared her throat, opened those formidable pipes she had on her, and yelled, "Hey, bird! What do you want from us?!"

For the first time since it had landed on Vesta's windowsill, the bird downed tools and showed an interest in the inhabitants of the room it was trying to break into.

"Yeah, just tell us what it is you want," Brutus added his two cents, also hollering at the top of his lungs, which, like Harriet's, were quite formidable.

The bird now cocked its head, as birds often do, and prefaced any remarks it intended to make by giving Vesta the benefit of a lengthy stare. Then it finally gave them the benefit of the sound of its voice by declaring something that Vesta didn't understand since she didn't speak the creature's language.

She turned to Harriet. "What did it say?"

"I think it wants you to open the window."

"But then it will fly away," said Vesta. "Won't it?"

Brutus shrugged. "I got the same message," he confessed.

And since a full quorum had given her the go-ahead, Vesta stalked over to the window and opened it. She shouldn't have been afraid the bird would take flight. Instead, it hopped onto the windowsill and glanced around the room. When its beady eyes landed on Harriet and Brutus, it seemed to puff out its chest and launched into a long harangue of words that came across as a lot of chirruping. When finally the stream of chirps dried up, Vesta saw that Harriet and Brutus sat looking up at the bird with looks of surprise etched on their furry faces.

"Well?" she asked. "What does it want? Tell me already!"

Brutus cleared his throat. "It says that..." He glanced uncertainly in Harriet's direction, but the Persian, contrary to her habit, seemed to have been struck dumb.

"What?" Vesta prompted. She was still holding on to her pencil, and if someone didn't start talking soon, she had a good mind to prod them with said pencil.

Finally, it was Harriet who spoke. She glanced up at Vesta with those remarkable green eyes of hers and said, "The bird wants you to cease and desist."

"Cease and desist? Cease and desist what?" She hated it when people spoke in riddles, and that applied to cats and birds, too.

"Cease and desist turning your backyard into a dead zone," said Brutus.

"And the front yard, too," said Harriet.

"I don't get it," she admitted. "My backyard isn't a dead

zone. It's full of flowers and plants and all manner of greenery!" If there was anything she prided herself in, it was the fact that she possessed a green thumb.

"You use too many pesticides," Brutus said. "Causing all the worms to take a hike. And worms being a principal food source for birds, you're depriving this poor bird and all of its friends of sustenance."

The bird launched into a series of chirrups once more, with Harriet and Brutus listening intently. "It also says you have to convince your neighbors to stop using pesticides," said Harriet.

"But most importantly," said Brutus. "It wants you and that neighborhood watch of yours to stop the development of Blake's field."

Now *that* Vesta could understand. The field that ran behind her house—and all the houses of their neighbors—had, in recent years, been allowed to turn into a minor jungle, with weeds and all manner of life allowed to spring up in wild abandon, no doubt becoming a haven for the local bird population. But now that Blake Carrington had given the go-ahead for the piece of land to be sold off and put into development, it wouldn't be long before that was all a thing of the past, with devastating consequences for all the species that lived there.

"There isn't a lot I can do about that," she said. "Blake sold the land, and the new owner seems intent on getting rid of what he calls an eyesore." Most of their neighbors were glad that the field would finally yield to a more aesthetically pleasing development, and everyone was hoping for a nice set of condos that would considerably raise the value of their own properties.

"Clark says you have to stop the development," Harriet reiterated. "In fact, he says that you're his last hope."

Now this was more to Vesta's liking. She often got the

impression that she was the only one who valued the existence of their neighborhood watch, but clearly there were others who thought the same thing—even if those others were of the feathered variety. "I'm afraid I don't know very much about it," she said. "All I know is that the field was sold off. I don't know anything about the new owner."

Brutus gave her a keen look. "So maybe it's time you found out, Gran?"

"After all, if they erect some tall building, it will make a big difference for all of us," Harriet argued. "Or imagine if they build a noisy factory? Or a wall?"

She shivered. The thought had occurred to her, but seeing as life had kept her pretty busy of late, she hadn't really looked into the sale of Blake's field yet. So she turned to the bird. "Clark, is it?"

The bird nodded. Or at least she thought it did.

"I'll look into the sale of the field," she said. "But I can't promise you that what I find will make you happy. And I can't promise that I'll be able to stop any development plans that might be harmful to your species."

"What about the pesticides, Gran?" asked Harriet. "You know you shouldn't use those. It's probably bad for us, too." She gave Vesta a reproachful look that spoke volumes.

"But I don't use pesticides!" she assured her audience. And even if she did, what harm could it do? All of it was approved by the EPA, as far as she knew. But as the bird kept giving her the evil eye and causing her to feel antsy, she finally caved. "Oh, fine," she said, throwing up her hands. "I'll see what I can do, all right?"

"And you will talk to the neighbors?" Brutus insisted.

"I will talk to the neighbors," she said. Though she didn't think they'd roll over and comply as easily as she just had. And all because of one stupid bird!

The bird chirped again, and Harriet smiled and said,

"Clark says thank you, and he will be following your future progress with considerable interest."

Somehow, and she didn't know why, she felt that there was more than a hint of menace in those words. But then she shrugged it off and gave the bird a quick nod. Clark seemed to return the nod and then spread his wings and flew off.

Chapter Two

Ronnie Vincent stared up at the ceiling and admired the brave and enterprising little spider that had attached itself to the corner of the molding. Lying next to his wife, he didn't stir, for fear of waking her up and causing her to turn over and pepper him with questions about his intentions, as she had done incessantly since he had told her the news. It wasn't that he didn't have the answers she was looking for, but more that he didn't want to get embroiled in another argument. After all, even though his intentions were pure, it was obvious that Lorie didn't exactly agree with him in that regard.

He should have known that when he launched this latest venture of his there would be pushback and plenty of wailing and gnashing of teeth. But he hadn't foreseen that it would be his own wife who would be most vocal amongst that crowd of naysayers and vehement critics of his work. He had tried to explain that he was doing it all for them—for the future of their family and most importantly for their kids, Sophie and Hannah. But it had all been for naught. Clearly Lorie had entirely different notions of what that future should look like, and it certainly didn't include the plans he had in mind.

He now placed his hands underneath his head and closed his eyes, as he gave himself up to thought. After all, it wasn't every day that you got the chance to change the world. To make it over in your own image. From scratch, as it were. As if yours was effectively the hand of God making tabula rasa and rummaging around with all creation. He grimaced. Lorie had accused him of harboring delusions of grandeur, and as he listened to his own thoughts, he wondered if she didn't have a point. To think he was God! Oh, the hubris!

The sleeping form of his wife stirred, and for a moment he held his breath. The last thing he needed was for another argument to ensue. He had enough on his plate as it was without trouble in the home adding to the list. But when her even breathing continued unabated, he soon relaxed. This was the moment that the tiny spider suddenly decided to take the great leap into the beyond and started abseiling from the ceiling, practically touching his face as it did. For a moment he fully thought it was going to land on his face and use it as a launch platform for further adventures. But as he watched the spider, his eyes going cross-eyed as he did, the spider must have become aware of the danger that lurked beneath and quickly reeled itself in and raced back up to the ceiling, where it was safe from harm and where no doubt it hoped to snatch a couple of fat flies as harbingers of great meals to come. Ronnie closed his eyes and dreamed of bigger things and the success of his venture, and soon he was fast asleep himself.

At least until a minor earthquake shook him to his foundations. When he opened his eyes, he saw that the earthquake consisted of their two daughters, Hannah and Sophie, and they were using his belly as a trampoline, as they often did. The noise they produced was enough to wake up an elephant, and since he and Lorie weren't denizens of that ancient and noble species, it didn't take them long to be fully awake. And as they gazed into each other's eyes while their offspring settled in between them, he wondered what his wife was thinking. For some reason, he had the impression she still wasn't very happy with him right now.

But that couldn't be helped. Whether she liked his plans or not, he was still going ahead with them.

The die was cast, and it was too late to put the genie back in the bottle.

* * *

Brenton Brooke darted a quick look left and right, then proceeded to cross the street at a trot, as was his habit. As a kid, his pop had always told him that traffic was a killer, and that you had to approach it like you did a wild beast of the jungle: by making sure you never allowed it to catch you unawares. And so he still made sure no car could ever come anywhere close to his person and run him over, as that particular species seemed to be in the habit of doing. A great big hulking monster of a vehicle honked its horn, and if he was startled, he didn't give any indication. He simply put more pep in his step and, not unlike a ballerina, performed a sort of pirouette in midair and made sure he was safely on the sidewalk before the vehicle could chew up parts of his person and maul him to death between its slathering jaws.

He gazed up at the facade of the building, and for a moment hesitated about whether he should set foot inside or not. But then he screwed up his courage to the sticking point and placed one foot on the threshold, a hand firmly on the knocker, and gave the implement a vigorous shake. Moments later, the sturdy door was yanked open by a liveried and bearded specimen that he surmised was some species of butler, so he stated his case. The underling listened without giving any indication that there was life behind the impassive facade but then deigned to step aside and allow him entry into the abyss. And so it was, with a beating heart and bated breath, that he placed himself into the hands of fate by entering the lair of Edmond Orbell, the eminent physician who came highly recommended by anyone dealing with the affliction that currently held him in its grip. After all, if Doctor Orbell couldn't see his way to returning him to full health, no one could.

Moments later, he was seated in the medical miracle worker's waiting room, where he found himself in the company of no fewer than three other patients, picked up a copy of Physician's Weekly from the salon table, and pretended to wait patiently for his turn. In actual fact, anxiety now held him firmly in its grip. And try as he might, he couldn't escape the notion that he may have made a mistake by placing his fate in the hands of Doctor Orbell.

One by one, the other inhabitants of the waiting room were called away by a friendly-looking nurse, and then finally, it was his turn. He rose from the plush and comfortable chair, replaced the copy of the medical journal on the table, and meekly followed the nurse down the corridor. She led him into the inner sanctum of Edmond Orbell's emporium and told him to take a seat while adding those time-honored words, "The doctor will see you soon," then silently closed the door.

Oddly enough, she hadn't even told him to take off all of his clothes, except for his socks and underwear. Not that he was upset about that, as he wasn't in the habit of taking off his clothes in the presence of ladies he had never met before. He might be a lot of things, but most of all he was a gentleman, and what was more, a gentleman who was faithful to his one true love, now more or less patiently sitting at home awaiting further proceedings. For he wasn't the only one who was anxious about what the day would bring.

Before long, the door opened and closed again, and as a man of voluminous aspect and dressed in a white smock strode in, a stethoscope dangling from his impressive neck, he knew he was in the presence of medical greatness.

"Mr... Brooke," he said, reading from the file he carried. And as he took a seat behind his desk, he gave him the benefit of a wintry smile. "So what can I do for you, Mr. Brooke?"

Which was his cue to turn from a normal human being into a blubbering mess of a man in just about two seconds flat, possibly setting a new world record.

Chapter Three

For some reason I couldn't quite comprehend, I found myself on the floor of the bedroom where I like to spend my nights. Under normal circumstances, I sleep at the foot of the bed that I share with my human Odelia and her husband Chase. Now though, try as I might, I couldn't remember how I had ended up on the floor next to the bed instead of in my usual spot. The only thing I could think was that Odelia must have had a nightmare and had kicked out with her feet, propelling me from the bed and landing my tush on the floor.

Lucky for me, Odelia has had the foresight of placing a small carpet next to the bed to protect her bare feet from the cold hardwood floor, and it was on this carpet that I now found myself, bemused and befuddled.

I glanced up at the bed, but nothing stirred, so whatever had caused me to fall from that great height, it was all in the past now. Even though I tried to search my memory, nothing presented itself as a possible explanation.

"You jumped down all by yourself, Max," suddenly a voice rang out not that far from me. When I glanced in the direction of the sound, I discovered that Grace, Odelia and

Chase's little girl, was looking at me intently from the safety of her cot.

"I jumped down?" I asked.

"I saw you do it," said the blond-haired little angel as she studied her fingernails. ""Twas the middle of the night, and not a creature stirred when all of a sudden you uttered a strange sound and jumped from the bed."

"What sound?" I asked, intrigued by this story.

She frowned. "Eeek," she said. "If memory serves."

"Eeek?"

"That's right. It sounded as if you were having a nightmare. I remember thinking something must have scared you because knowing you, it takes a lot to elicit such a sound. So whatever you were dreaming of, it must have been pretty terrifying." She shivered. "Please tell me what it was, Max. Was it very horrible?"

It's a trait I've noticed in many a human person: this obsession with the macabre and the ghoulish. On the one hand, they profess to hate scary things, but on the other, they love it. It's a quirk I don't share with them, I have to admit. For me, scary is scary, and however you choose to look at it, it never becomes fun.

"I don't remember," I confessed. "I don't even remember how I ended up down here instead of up there."

"A nightmare," she said, nodding confidently. "And a very scary one."

A third voice now joined the conversation. It was my good friend and housemate Dooley, and as he stuck his head over the edge of the bed and gazed down into the precipice, he looked pretty scared himself, I have to say. "Was it very terrible, Max?" he asked. "This nightmare you had? What was it about? Were there monsters? Was there..." He shook violently. "Was there a giant spider?!"

"Like I just told Grace, I don't remember having a night-

EXCERPT FROM PURRFECT VIRUS (MAX 79)

mare," I told my fluffy-haired feline friend. "All I know is that I woke up just now and found myself on the floor."

"On the rug," Grace corrected me. She always was a stickler for *le mot juste*.

"On the rug," I agreed, giving her the benefit of a grateful smile.

"Pity I can't look into your head," she said now. "And see what your nightmare was about."

Now it was my turn to shiver violently. Imagine if people started looking into your head and reading your mind. Now, wouldn't that be a most terrifying thing?

"I'm sure it was nothing," I told her. "Just one of those things, you know."

"Indigestion," said Dooley. "It often leads to bad dreams. What did you eat last night, Max? Was it something heavy? I'll bet that's what made you suffer that nightmare you had."

I didn't recall having eaten a heavy meal. Just a few nuggets of food as usual. As a rule, I don't like to eat before retiring for the night, since I hate falling asleep with a full stomach. But try as I might, I couldn't convince Dooley that his theory wasn't accurate. So finally I decided to drop it. The topic bored me already.

"I dreamed of my first day of school," said Grace, a beatific smile on her face now. "I can't wait to start school, you guys. Meet a lot of great friends. Meet the person who's going to take me by the hand and lead me to the world of grown-ups. Who will transfer all of her wisdom and knowledge to me and fill my head with wonder and the miracle of enlightenment. It's one of those watershed moments in any young person's life that I, for one, can't wait to launch into."

Dooley and I both stared at the kid. "That's... great," I said, a little lamely, I must admit. For some reason, I had a feeling that reality might not live up to the dream. Though of course it was entirely possible that she met such a wonderful teacher who would usher in a world of wonder, erudition, culture, and intellect. As it was, she was already a lot smarter than I was, even at her young age.

She now glanced out of the window, located next to her cot. Sunlight was starting to seep in, and as she took in the new dawn, she said, "You guys, something's going on in Blake's field."

"Yeah, rumor has it that the field has been sold," I told her. "So it looks like they'll be turning it into something other than a derelict piece of wasteland."

"Diggers have arrived," she said. "And if I'm not mistaken, they're going to start digging a very big hole any moment now."

Dooley and I shared another look, this time of alarm. "But I thought they were going to turn it into a park?" said my friend. "Do they need diggers to create a park, Max?"

"I'm sure they do," I said. "They need to get rid of all those weeds and bushes and the ramshackle structures that have sprung up over there. So diggers are probably the best way to go."

Dooley relaxed and placed his head on his paws. "I like parks. Parks are nice. Kids playing, people relaxing, birds chirping... Maybe we can even move cat choir to this new park. That way we don't have to walk so far at night."

"Yeah, that would be a good idea," I said. Though I wasn't sure our neighbors would necessarily agree. For some reason, humans don't often appreciate the artistic contribution a cat choir makes to the world of music.

And I would have closed my eyes for a quick little nap when suddenly Brutus and Harriet burst into the room. "You guys!" Harriet yelled. "They're going to turn Blake's field into a factory!"

"Or a wall!" said Brutus.

"Or an ugly office tower!"

Odelia, who had finally woken up from all the noise, muttered sleepily, "What's with all the racket?"

"The field, Odelia!" said Brutus. "Some developers are going to build the Empire State Building right next to our home—and we have to stop them!"

In a flash, I suddenly remembered what my nightmare had been about: for some reason, I had found myself falling into a deep, dark, bottomless pit!

ABOUT NIC

Nic has a background in political science and before being struck by the writing bug worked odd jobs around the world (including but not limited to massage therapist in Mexico, gardener in Italy, restaurant manager in India, and Berlitz teacher in Belgium).

When he's not writing he enjoys curling up with a good (comic) book, watching British crime dramas, French comedies or Nancy Meyers movies, sampling pastry (apple cake!), pasta and chocolate (preferably the dark variety), twisting himself into a pretzel doing morning yoga, going for a run, and spoiling his big red tomcat Tommy.

He lives with his wife (and aforementioned cat) in a small village smack dab in the middle of absolutely nowhere and is probably writing his next 'Mysteries of Max' book right now.

www.nicsaint.com